# Darkness of Umbra University

Ella Kyle

Published by Ella Kyle, 2024.

DARKNESS OF UMBRA UNIVERSITY

**First edition. February 13, 2024.**

Copyright © 2024 Ella Kyle.

ISBN: 979-8224876822

Written by Ella Kyle.

To my younger self, who loved creating stories

# Chapter 1

The kidnapper has a knife to Emily's throat. I can't move my body. I can't do anything but watch. Watch as the brown-haired bearded man is threatening my sister's life. I'm stuck. My mind is racing with a list of things I can do to help her. If I could find a way to move, maybe I could try throwing something at him. But all that is around me are tall green trees and dirt. I could throw a stick at him. Or I could throw my shoe at the kidnapper to distract him while I grab Emily. But none of them work. All I can do is stand there, watching the horror in my sister's eyes as I stand here, motionless.

"Blue, help me! How could you let him do this to me, to your sister? How could you let him take me? You are supposed to protect me. He is going to kill me if you keep standing there!" Emily yells. Tears are falling down her face.

"I'm sorry Emily. I c-can't move," I tell her. I'm crying, sobbing more like it. I try to use my earth powers, but I can't. Damn zodiac power. So useless when I need it the most.

"Don't let them kill me! Please help me!" Emily screams.

It's happening. My greatest fear is happening. He is going to kill her, and there is nothing I can do.

"I'm trying!" I try to move again, but I still can't. I can't bear this. It's too much.

"Looks like you can't save your little sister after all. What a wimp," the kidnapper smiles a devil's smile. I hate him. I hate him for taking my sister from me. I hate him for doing this to me. That's not what I tell him though, instead, I say

*"Please don't hurt her. Take me instead, please!" I beg.*

*"Sorry, but no can do. You'll just have to watch the light vanish from her eyes instead." I watch as the kidnapper pushes the blade harder into Emily's throat. Emily lets out a frightened whimper. I swallow hard to keep myself from throwing up right here. I can't take this. I can't lose Emily.*

*"Blue," her voice sounds so innocent, this shouldn't be happening to my little sister. She is crying harder now. I hate it when she cries, I hate it.*

*Somehow the kidnapper's smile grows wider. This can't be happening. I can't breathe. Then the kidnapper slices Emily's throat. I watch as her lifeless body falls to the ground. Blood spills onto the floor from her body. She lays there, motionless.*

*"EMILY!" I yell.*

I jerk awake screaming. I'm going to be sick. My whole body is sweating, my hair is sticking to the back of my neck. I can feel the tears that are falling down my cheek. I need to get my breathing under control.

*BOOM*

I get so scared that it feels like my soul jumps out of my body. Once I'm less startled I look across my room and out my window to find that it's raining. It was just thunder that woke me up. I'm okay, it was just a dream. Just a dream. The clock on my nightstand says it's 4:00 am. My tears are slowing down. My vision isn't as blurry anymore. I leave for Umbra University in a few hours. The place where I decide what will happen in my future. Where I decide what I'll do for the rest of my life. I fall back down on my bed. It's not like I don't want to go, I do. I just don't like the thought of leaving Emily. Emily, who I just watched die in front of me. Breathe. It was just a dream. Emily, Emily is-

"Blue?"

Emily is peeking her head through my door. Her wavy light brown hair, almost dirty blonde, like mine, falling in front of her face. She's okay. She wasn't taken. She is still here. There is a look of concern in her blue eyes. Emily has blue eyes like my mother, while I have brown eyes like my father.

"Y-Yes," I reply.

"I thought I heard you scream. Are you alright?" Emily asks.

"I'm fine. Just a nightmare, that's all." My eyes must be red and puffy. It's a good thing it is dark so she can't see.

She walks into my room and climbs in bed with me. I wrap my arms around her and hold her tight. Hugging her always brings me comfort. She makes me feel safe. She is the reason I am the person I am today. I don't know who I would be without her.

"Do you want to talk about it?" Emily asks. By the tone of her voice I know she is still concerned.

I take a deep breath. "It was just my fear of losing you," I tell her. Tears are threatening to fall again. I can't cry, not in front of her. I have to stay strong.

She is silent for a moment. Her ocean blue eyes watch me. Then she wraps her arms around me and hugs me tight.

"It's okay Blue. You won't lose me, okay?" She tries to reassure me.

"Okay," My fear is still there. It'll always be there. It's a fear I can't really get rid of, but I know Emily is trying her best to calm me down.

I kiss her on the forehead before falling asleep. The sound of thunder is booming in the background while rain hits the window. Emily's body is warm against mine as I drift off. I will wake up in a few more hours to go to a place that will change my life forever. That thought makes my nerves spark up.

# Chapter 2

I gather up my things from my room and head downstairs. I was able to get about three more hours of sleep before I had to wake up again. I tried not to disturb Emily in the process of getting ready, but I failed. Once she was up, I told her to go get dressed. After she left, I finished packing up my things and got ready for the day.

Heading downstairs, I could already smell the bacon and eggs my mom is cooking. She always wakes up early and makes breakfast for me and my sister. It's almost like a tradition.

"Good morning honey," My mom beams at me.

"Morning Mom," I say, still sleepy. I'm not a morning person. I always stay up late reading or sometimes studying. My sister and I will occasionally watch a movie on the tv in my room. My parents never like it when Emily stays up too late so we would always have to be quiet while watching the movie. I walk over to the kitchen table and find a place to sit.

From where I sit, I can see the whole kitchen area. When you walk through our open door, it leads you to a big open room. The kitchen table sits in the bottom right corner of the room. The kitchen area is in the upper right area of the room. White kitchen counters line the walls. The island sits in between the kitchen and the table, making it so it separates the two areas. The island is a bunch of counters that form the shape of a rectangle. We have stools set at the side closest to the table so we can sometimes sit there and eat. Though I usually sit on the bar stools, today I wanted to sit at the table in hopes my family would join me for my last morning here. It's crazy how I will be leaving soon.

To the left of the kitchen is the living room area with the couch and tv. My mom has a bookshelf on the far left wall, she has always loved to read. A little to the right of the bookshelf is where the stairs that lead upstairs are and to the right of those are the stairs that go down to the basement. At the far end of the wall is the bathroom. All of our bedrooms are upstairs.

My mom walks over to me with a plate full of food and puts it down in front of me. "I thought I would make you breakfast one last time before you go to Umbra University. I can't believe it, you're already nineteen. My little baby's all grown up and now you're leaving me."

I take a bite of some eggs before answering. "Mom, you know I am not going to be gone forever. Just a couple of years. Then I'll come back to Prusmé and we can all go boating on the lake like old times. Besides, I'll still come and visit when I can,"

My parents both grew up in Prusmé. They spent practically all of their time in the water. Boating, swimming, anything you can think of, they were doing. Then, they met at a restaurant one day and took a liking to each other. Obviously, they got married and had Emily and me. Their beautiful angels, as they like to call us. Now we all go swimming and boating on the lake together.

"I know, I was just teasing you," She laughed then headed back over to the stove to clean up. She's definitely anxious. "I will miss you though and I want you to call me, okay?" She scrubs down the stove while talking to me. I know she is nervous about me leaving, you can tell by how frantically she is cleaning everything she can. Whenever she gets nervous or anxious, I start to feel the same way. It is scary to think that I will be on my own and I can't rely on my parents as much.

"I will. It'll be different without you guys there but I still have Harley. Even though she is a Taurus and we will be in different dorms, we will still hang out a lot. Hopefully." I grab some bacon from my plate and stuff it into my mouth as I think about Harley, who has been my best friend since childhood.

"You will. When I went to the university, I still saw my friends a lot. But you have to make sure you focus on your work too. Keep practicing with your earth powers." She moves on to rinsing the dishes and drying them with a towel.

"I will make sure I focus and practice."

When everyone in the Andagar Realms turns nineteen they go to Umbra University for two years. Umbra University is a place similar to a school, but we learn more things to help us with our future. Once you arrive you get separated by your zodiac sign for living arrangements, but classes are not separated by your sign. Everyone can attend regardless of their sign. Each zodiac has a different dorm building and there are two buildings for each sign, one for girls and one for boys. We go to training class which helps us learn more about our powers and how to control them. It also teaches us how to use weapons. Being a Capricorn means I have earth powers. I can make balls out of dirt and throw them at people or objects, which is my favorite thing to do. I can even-

"Hello!" I turn around and see Harley come through the door. She has curled the tips of her long brown hair, obviously getting dressed up for the occasion. It's as if the sun is lined up perfectly so when it hits her blue eyes, it looks like they sparkle. Her full lips and pearly white teeth are in the shape of a big grin. She always loves the dramatic entrance. Maybe I should've dressed up more and done my hair too. All I did was comb my messy bed head and put on a comfy sweater. Oh well, it's not like I'm trying to impress anyone. Harley is always trying to get guys' attention. "Who's ready to head on out of here and go party and meet some boys?" I'm just about finished with my breakfast so we will have to leave the house soon.

"Now Harley, you know it's not all about meeting boys and partying. It's about helping you get ready for your future," my mom tells Harley.

Harley and I have been best friends ever since we were little. Our parents know each other from childhood so we basically grew up together. Harley and her family live just down the street. Sometimes our families go boating together, the kids swim in the lake while the adults drink on the boat. Obviously the driver doesn't, who is usually my dad.

One time, when Harley had a boyfriend named Kent, he came with us out on the lake. The ride out was a little awkward because Harley's dad kept staring intensely at Kent. Let's just say that her dad was never a big fan of him. Kent ended up breaking up with Harley a few months later because he was interested in someone else. Her dad was not happy about that.

Harley takes a seat at the table. "I know," Harley sighs. My mom gives her an approving smile. Harley has basically grown up as a part of our family. My parents are like her second parents or "bonus" parents. There is never a weekend where Harley isn't around. Some people may think it gets annoying always having her here, but I don't. I enjoy the company.

"We can still have fun *while* studying," I assure Harley. She just sighs and picks up the news article that was on the table.

My mom walks over and places a plate full of food in front of Harley. "Why do people always like to read the news? I can't get past this first paragraph." Harley puts a big mouthful of food in her mouth. I can't help but laugh.

Harley looks over at me, food still stuffed in her mouth. "What?" she asks.

I laugh some more. "Nothing." There is still a smile on my face when she looks away.

"People read the news to know what is going on in the world. It is always good to read it occasionally," Mom answers. She rests her hands on the island and takes a deep breath. She looks around the kitchen, probably looking for something else to clean.

We continue to eat for a little bit longer until we realize the time. When I finish my breakfast, Emily joins us downstairs. "You guys have to get going if you don't want to be late," my mother says.

We both help clean up the dishes from breakfast and put them in the dishwasher. Harley then helps me gather my stuff and put it in her car outside. I turn around and Emily comes running up and hugs me.

"You have to call me every day okay? And you have to visit us, or at least me. I can't believe you'll be at oo-m-bruh university," She has a hard time pronouncing Umbra University, I don't know why. It's not like she finds lots of words hard to say.

"Emily, you know I won't forget you, mom or dad. Also, I probably won't be able to call you *every day,* but I'll call often," I reply.

The front door opens and Dad walks outside. He is starting to get some gray hairs in his short brown hair. His beard is even growing in too. He has on his worn-down jeans and red flannel shirt. "Where have you been?" I ask him.

"I was working in the garage." He walks up and gives me one of his bear hugs. I feel mom and Emily's arms wrap around me soon after.

"Don't forget about me!" Harley comes crashing into the hug. We all start to laugh.

We all let go and say our goodbyes. Once I climb into the passenger seat of Harley's car, I look out the window and see Emily and my mom start to cry. My dad is never the one to cry, at least not in front of others. I wave goodbye to my family one last time as we head down my driveway. I watch as our two-story lake house disappears behind us. I'm going to miss the house, my family and Prusmé but I know I'll make lots of memories at the university.

It will be different not having Emily around. When I'm having a tough day, all Emily has to do is smile to make me feel better. Even though we are eight years apart, we still get along well. Most people I know with big age gaps between their siblings don't get along as well and they aren't as close.

"I am *so* glad I don't have to worry about my parents riding on my back anymore. They're always like *'You better be studying and not partying all the time'* or *'We are expecting you to be getting good grades, Harley.'* Like oh my god, just let me live my life!" Harley complains.

"I understand how you could be enjoying this right now," I say, Harley's comment making me chuckle.

"Umbra University, here we come," I say.

# Chapter 3

We arrived at Umbra University hours later, stopping at the wall surrounding the campus. The guards make us show the badges we received in the mail earlier this week, which allow us to get into Umbra University. The guards then grant us access and we drive on in. Harley pulls the car into the parking area and finds an open spot.

We get out of the car and grab our bags and once again I think how bummed I am that Harley and I aren't staying in the same dorm building. Since Harley is a Taurus and I am a Capricorn we have separate buildings, but thankfully the dorms are close to each other.

Walking past the Sagittarius dorms, we see that students are outside playing around with their firepower. They make shapes with the fire like hearts and stick figures. It reminds me of playing with sparklers while boating one summer. The Sagittarius students wear purple uniforms, indicating what zodiac they are. I always thought that having the firepower would be a pretty cool power to have. You just need lots of control or you could burn a whole building down. I would not want to get in trouble for doing something like that.

We finally get to the front of my dorm building where they separate the boys and girls into two different dorm buildings. The dorms are made out of faded red bricks. Above the front door is a zodiac symbol, depending on which dorm building it is. The symbol for my dorm building is the Capricorn symbol, it almost looks like an "N" with a loop on the end.

"Hey, Ash!" A kid goes running by, cutting me and Harley off.

"Watch where you are going you-" Harley starts to squeal. Yes, a freaking squeal. "Oh my gosh, Blue, It's Asher King!" Harley nudges me with her elbow.

"Ow," I look over and see who Harley is talking about. The boy looks about 6'0 with a lean body. He has brown tossed hair, but it looks lighter in the sunlight. I skim over his long straight nose and full lips. If I am being honest, he does look kind of cute.

"Asher? Who is Asher King?" I ask while still looking him over. He is surrounded by a group of girls, showing off his powers. I wonder what sign he is? He doesn't have on a uniform to say what he is, but he is obviously one of the firepower signs.

"He is just a really hot guy I follow online," Harley replies.

"You follow a stranger on Instagram. He isn't even a celebrity," I mention, giving Harley a strange look.

"He's no stranger, he's Asher King!"

I roll my eyes at her and look back at Asher, who is now showing all the girls how he juggles fireballs. Ridiculous. I internally laugh at the sight of him and think to myself he looks like a stuck-up showoff. Not that I have any room to judge. He could just look that way. "Never judge a book by its cover" is what my mom would always preach to us growing up, so I know I shouldn't judge Asher King by what he looks like on the outside.

Harley is still watching Asher. She has the same look as all the girls that are surrounding him. Oh god Harley, couldn't you have chosen someone who isn't surrounded by his fan girls? You could do better than him.

"He is just juggling fire, you can just go to a show and watch that stuff. Let's go." I grab Harley's arm and pull her in the direction of our dorms, trying not to drop my stuff at the same time.

I STAND OUTSIDE MY dorm room, fumbling for the keys that I received last week with the rest of my orientation information. The university sends you a key for your dorm room before you arrive. I finally unlock the door and push it open. It is a four-walled room with two beds pushed up against the wall on either side. A window sits in-between the middle of the beds. There is a dresser at the end of each bed and a night stand sits at the head of both of the beds by the window. It looks like my roommate has already arrived because she has her stuff set up on the left side of the room, but she is nowhere to be found.

I walk inside and start unpacking my things. Before Harley left for her dorm, she told me to meet her outside for lunch at twelve. We are going to look at places to eat in town. It is already eleven-thirty so I only have thirty minutes to unpack.

When I open up the dresser to put my clothes away, I see my uniform lying there neatly folded. Before we arrive at the university, we have to send them some information about us like name and zodiac sign, basic things like that. They also ask us for clothing sizes for our uniforms.

For the girl's uniform, we have a nice black suit jacket. Under the jacket, we wear a white long sleeve button-up shirt. The uniform also requires a skirt that is a tinted shade of our zodiac color. The skirt stops above my kneecap. When it gets cold, we are allowed to wear black tights under our skirts. Even though they don't seem like much help, at least we have something. We also have to wear long black socks with nice black shoes. The shoes are sitting on the floor next to my dresser. I touch the fabric of my nice brown skirt. I was worried that my uniform was going to be a crappy shade of brown, but looking at it now, it doesn't seem that bad.

For the guy's uniform, they also wear a black suit jacket with a white button-up shirt underneath. Since the guys don't wear a skirt for their uniform, they have a tie instead to show their zodiac color. Then they wear nice black pants with black socks and shoes. The guys also have another option of wearing a cream-colored sweater vest with a long sleeve white button-up shirt underneath. They would still wear a tie and instead of black pants, they would have cream-colored pants to match the sweater.

After I finish unpacking, I change into my uniform and head outside. It isn't freezing outside right now, though it is getting cooler. I really don't feel like walking in the cold. Harley must still be unpacking because she isn't outside. On the lawn in front of my dorm there are a bunch of boys playing a game of football. Looking more closely, I can see Asher is amongst them. As if he knows someone is watching, he looks over and catches me staring at him.

*Shit*

I quickly look away hoping he doesn't notice. I have a feeling he did. I slowly look back and see Asher smirking at me. Great, he did notice. I give him an annoyed look in return which just makes his smirk grow wider. I can't have him thinking I'm another one of his fangirls, but I don't want to be the first to look away either, so I keep staring at him. He just stares back. As I look at him I notice he has his uniform on now. He has a red tie so that means he is an Aries. His friends are calling him so he will have to look away soon and if he-

"Blue!" Harley calls. I look away to find Harley coming my way. She is wearing her uniform but instead of a brown skirt, hers is a tinted green color. I look back over at Asher who has a smug look on his face. He walks over to his friends and slaps one on the back before they start talking. Damn it, now he has won. Next time I won't be the first to look away. Wait no, there will be no next time. He is just a stuck-up guy who I want nothing to do with. What the hell is wrong with me?

Harley walks up to me. "You okay?" She looks over to see what I am looking at. "Ooo you looking at the cute guys over there?" She nudges me.

"No. Well, yes I am. But I mean, it's not like that," I stutter. Why the hell did I just stutter? I never do that.

"Then what is it like," Harley says sarcastically while giving me a big grin. I struggle to find the right words to say back.

"You know what? Never mind. Let's go," I walk away irritated that Harley thinks that and, if I'm honest, that Asher won the staring contest thingy or whatever it was.

We walk to the other side of the campus to a place called Corner Cafe located in town. When we walk in, we order our food and drinks at the counter in the back. Once they give us our drinks, we pick out a table and wait for our food.

"Have you met your roommate yet?" Harley asks me while taking a sip of her mocha.

"No, have you?" I ask.

"Yeah, her name is Adeline. She seems pretty cool. I mean, I only just met her but I have a feeling I'm going to take a liking to her,"

"You better like her because you will be living with her for the year," I say sarcastically. The thing about our roommates is that the university picks who we live with. So we just have to hope for the best. You can obviously contact the resident advisor if there are any problems, but they won't always let you change rooms.

She rolls her eyes then takes a sip of her drink. "Harley Moore," a worker calls. Harley gets up and grabs our food. She comes back to the table and we begin to eat.

"This looks so good," Harley comments. We both got the spinach salad. She takes out a packet of ranch and spreads it on her salad.

When we finish up our lunch, I look up at the clock and realize the time. "We should probably head to the campus buildings. We need to pick up our schedules."

We both quickly clean up whatever is left of our lunch and head out the door. When walking to the campus buildings, I noticed that more students have arrived since we've been here. More people are walking around the campus grounds and it really is making this feel real...we are really here!

Inside the campus buildings, there is a table set up at the entrance with a line that backs up all the way to the doors we came through. After about twenty minutes of waiting, it is finally our turn. Harley walks up to the table first and a lady sitting behind the table asks for her name.

"Harley Moore,"

The woman looks down and scans a piece of paper with a list of names on it. "Alright, you will head to room 136 on the first floor. There you will get your schedule and the staff will explain some things," the woman tells Harley.

I walk up to the desk after Harley is done and walks away. "Name?" The woman has her blonde hair put up in a fancy bun. She looks to be in her forties. I wonder if she is one of the professors here.

"Blue Layton."

She moves her finger down the paper. Her finger stops on a spot on the paper. "Ah, here we go. You will be in room 138, on the first floor. Down that hall." She directs me towards one of the hallways.

I thank her and walk over to Harley, who is waiting for me. We walk down the hall together, since the rooms we are assigned to are next to each other.

"Meet me back out here when you are done, we can see if we have any classes together," Harley tells me.

"Sounds good." I walk into room 138 and see there is another line that leads up to yet another table.

While waiting in line, I look around the room. There are rows and rows of long desks that curve a little in the middle. As the rows go farther back, the higher the tables are. There are aisles of stairs to help you get to a seat. Looking back at the line, I can tell it is going by quickly. I'm hoping Harley and I will have at least one class together. For most of our years at school back home, we weren't in that many classes together, so maybe we'll get lucky this year. At least there's the chance that someone from my high school in Prusmé could be in one of my classes.

Everyone in the line moves up a few steps. There are only about six people in front of me now. Someone taps my shoulder and I turn around to see a tall guy with darker skin, who looks to be around 5'11 standing behind me. His black hair is cut at a shorter length. His eyes, a pretty dark shade of blue, stare at me with curiosity in them. He has a long-hooked nose and nice full lips. His tie for his uniform is a lighter shade of blue, meaning he is a Libra. He smiles at me like he has known me his whole life.

"Hi. I'm Jupiter." The boy extends his hand out for me to shake.

Shaking his hand I say, "I'm Blue. It's nice to meet you."

When we stop shaking hands, Jupiter says, "It is nice to meet you too. You look lovely today, Blue."

"Oh uh, thank you so much. You look very nice today too," I reply, not expecting the compliment and awkwardly responding.

Jupiter's smile grows wider. "Thank you, I appreciate the compliment. I always like to give people little compliments because when they smile, it feels good to know you have brightened their day."

"That is very sweet. Well, it worked, my day is brightened." I give Jupiter a warm smile to match his.

"Well, that is good to hear. It looks like it is your turn now." I look behind me to find there is no one in front of me. I quickly walk up to the table and get my schedule. The staff member explains that all my classes are in the same two campus buildings except for my training class. That will be located at the training facility. Training class is where they work with us on our zodiac powers. They also teach us how to use swords, knives, and bows. While here, I also pick up a couple of textbooks that I pay for ahead of time.

As I go to leave, I tell Jupiter, "Hope to see you around." He says the same to me. I walk back into the hallway to find that Harley is not done yet. I wait against the wall so I am not in anyone's way. A bunch of people are walking down the halls, wearing all different color uniforms. It's cool to be able to tell people's zodiac by the color of their uniform.

Harley walks out of the room a couple minutes later. We head down the hall and out of the building. I don't feel as anxious anymore since I have gotten everything I need. Now all I have to do is go to my classes and study hard. That should be easy right? What am I thinking? I'm attending university classes.

"I met this guy named Jupiter while I was in line. He was super sweet. He complimented me and said the cutest thing about how he likes giving everyone compliments in hopes to make them smile. Maybe we'll get to see him around campus and I can introduce you," I tell Harley.

"That sounds better than my experience in line. All I did was stand there and wait, wait and *wait*. Not that there weren't any cute guys in line. They just didn't approach me, though I saw one guy eyeing me. I mean seriously, the guys here need to learn some confidence! Am I right? They need to learn how to be brave enough to walk up to a girl," Harley says.

"Harley, not all guys are going to talk to you." Harley looks at me with a confused expression. "It's not like you're not likable! I'm just saying they could have been focusing more on getting ready for their classes than talking to you. Plus, they may not have wanted to lose their spot in line."

"I know. I'm just jealous. I want this to be a fun experience, I don't want to be studying all the time," Harley explains to me.

"I understand but come on." I wrap my arm around her shoulder. "You're Harley Moore, you don't need some guy to make you happy."

Harley perks up and holds her chin up high. "You're right, I am Harley Moore. No man is ever as powerful as me." We laugh together as we walk back to our dorms.

# Chapter 4

We get back to my dorm after stopping at Harley's to drop off her textbooks. I still haven't met with my roommate. She must be out with her friends. Harley and I sit down on my bed and pull out our schedules. We put the papers side by side and compare them to each other.

"We have our first class together, history," Harley points out as my eyes continue to scan the small pieces of paper, going over the rest of our schedules.

"Actually, we have two classes together, history and training," I tell Harley. Thank goodness we have at least one. I was nervous we wouldn't have any together.

"That's better than none," Harley says. I take my schedule and fold it into my bag.

Suddenly the door to my dorm opens. A girl with white colored skin and short blonde wavy hair walks in. She has flushed bow-shaped lips and round blue eyes and curves in all the right places. She has on her brown Capricorn uniform, so I assume she must be my roommate. Well, how else would she have gotten in here? She has a shocked look on her face, I'm assuming because she probably didn't expect to see Harley and I in here.

"Oh, sorry if I'm interrupting. I'm Luna, your roommate." Luna puts her hand out for us to shake. If it wasn't for our uniforms, Luna probably wouldn't be able to tell who her roommate is.

I quickly stand up and shake her hand. "Hi, I'm Blue. It's nice to meet you." I signal to Harley and say, "This is my friend Harley."

Luna lets go of my hand and gives Harley a wave. "It is nice to meet you guys too," Luna says.

"Well, I better get going. I'll see you in class tomorrow." Harley gives me a hug then heads out the door. I look at the clock that is above the door and it's around 3:00pm in the afternoon.

"It is nice to meet you but my friends are waiting for me downstairs. I'll see you later though when I get back," Luna walks over to her nightstand and grabs a charger. "Sorry to be leaving so soon."

"You're fine, I understand." I give her a warm-hearted smile. She waves goodbye as she heads out the door.

I walk over to the bag I brought with me and pull out one of the few books I have. I plop down on my bed feeling a bit tired, but I didn't even do anything to make me feel this way. I guess it is from traveling here.

I spent the next hour reading. I look up at the clock and it tells me it's 4:30 pm. I take out my phone from my pocket and text Harley asking her if she wants to eat dinner together. A couple minutes later she texts me back saying she made plans with Adeline and her friends. She says I can tag along, but I don't want to intrude, so I decline the offer. I go back to reading my book since there is not much else I can do. I'm glad Harley is already making friends. It feels like it has always been easy for her, unlike me.

An hour later, I put on my shoes and head outside feeling bored. I walk over to the other side of campus to town. There are some restaurants and a small grocery store made out of the same material as the dorms. The shop owners live on the floor above their business, making it easier for them to just walk downstairs and open their shop instead of driving a long way. While I walk along the paved surface, I look at all of the places I can eat. As I get to the end, I see the cafe Harley and I ate lunch at. To the right of it there is a place called the Zodiac Grill. Sounds interesting. When I walk inside, one of the workers helps me to one of the booths by the far wall. The waiter hands me a menu then tells me they will be right back.

As I'm looking over the menu, someone calls my name. I look around the room and my eyes land on the entrance. Jupiter stands there with his Libra uniform waving at me. I wave back as he starts to walk towards me.

"Look who I caught at the Zodiac Grill," Jupiter says with a big smile on his face.

"I didn't expect to see you here. Did you come with someone?" I ask while looking around.

"No actually, I came here by myself. Are you here with someone?" he asks.

"Just me. Would you like to join?" I ask, motioning to the other side of the booth.

"Are you sure? I really don't want to intrude. I understand if you want to be alone, I can just go find another-"

"Just sit Jupiter," I interrupt while laughing.

He seems hesitant at first but decides to join me. He slides into the bench across from me. The Zodiac Grill seems pretty busy today, most of the tables are occupied. Waiters keep coming in and out of the kitchen, delivering food and drinks. Umbra University students tend to get jobs here. I'll have to look around to see if there is a place I would like to work at.

I hand Jupiter my menu and say, "Here, I already know what I want."

Jupiters takes the menu and thanks me. Soon the waiter comes back and takes both of our orders. Jupiter got the steakhouse burger while I got the BBQ ribs.

"I didn't take you as a rib kind of girl," Jupiter jokes.

"What is that supposed to mean?" I ask.

"I don't know. I just didn't see you as the kind of person to order ribs. You're more of a salad girl." We both start to laugh. It honestly feels nice to be laughing and hanging out with Jupiter. This would be fun to do more often.

"I did eat a salad for lunch today," I state.

"You do seem like more of a salad type of person."

The waiter brings our food and drinks out. We end up eating and talking for the next hour. When we are done, Jupiter offers to walk me back to my dorm. It is starting to get dark out and he doesn't like the idea of me being alone when there are drunk students walking around. It took me a bit of persuading, being that I don't know Jupiter that well, but I ended up accepting his offer.

On the way to my dorm building, we talked about our lives back home and our families. Jupiter said that he was born in Bonleno, but when his second younger sister was born, his parents decided to move to Litu. The snowy state as everyone likes to call it. Litu has these big mountains called the Frozen Summit. I visited Litu once. I thought it got pretty cold in Prusmé, but no way, definitely not compared to Litu. In Prusmé it occasionally snows and the lake gets frozen over and we can go ice-skating. But in Litu, there is always snow on the ground. I've been told that there is rarely a day when they don't have any snow. Just thinking of that makes me shiver. The cold is not for me.

"My sisters and I always love to go skiing and snowboarding. We have never gone skiing on the Frozen Summit, but there are places with smaller hills in Litu where we have been instead. They are still pretty steep, don't get me wrong, just not as steep as the Frozen Summit," Jupiter explains.

"I always wanted to try skiing. I never got the chance when I went to Litu for a vacation once. All we really did was go ice-skating or sled riding. I have tried snowboarding, but it wasn't really my thing. The vacation was still fun, but I really want to try skiing next time I visit," I tell him.

"Next time you visit you have to let me know. My sisters and I can help teach you," Jupiter says excitedly.

"I would love that."

We made it to my dorm pretty quickly. Time flies by when you're having fun. "Thank you so much for walking me back. I really appreciate it. Oh and thanks for joining me for dinner," I say.

"Thank you for *letting* me join you. Hope to see you around."

"You too. Be safe walking back," I say, concerned.

"I will," Jupiter turns around and heads back to his dorm.

I walk inside my dorm room and Luna is not back from hanging with her friends yet. Even though it is not even close to when I normally go to bed, I am already exhausted. I take off my shoes and collapse on my bed. I grab the blanket I brought and my book from my nightstand, then I start reading.

Luna eventually comes back around eight. I should probably go to sleep early so I have some good rest for tomorrow. I grab my pajama bottoms and a t-shirt, then head to the public bathroom where I brush my teeth and get ready for bed. There are five floors in each dorm and a public bathroom on each floor which makes it so there's not much overcrowding. It's nice not having people all up in my business.

Once I get back to my room, I tell Luna goodnight and turn off the light. When I am back in bed, I check to make sure my alarm is set so I don't sleep in. I also text Harley and my family goodnight. There is a faint glow on Luna's side of the room. She must be on her phone.

As I drift to sleep, I think about everything that is coming up. My life and the experiences I am going to have here. Before I know it, I am already asleep, dreaming about my future here at Umbra University.

# Chapter 5

I jerk awake to the sound of my alarm. Picking up my phone from the nightstand, I check the time. It's 9:00 am and I notice Luna isn't in her bed. She must be at one of her classes already. I have an hour until my first class starts, so I should probably leave at least ten-fifteen minutes early. The class starts at ten and being the first day I should probably be there at 9:50 am. I text Harley and let her know to be ready by 9:35 am so we can grab a quick breakfast.

I grab a new uniform from the dresser along with my basic essentials, like a toothbrush and toothpaste, a brush, things like that. When I get to the bathroom there are already people up and getting ready for their day. I wait a few minutes for a stall to become available. Once one frees up, I quickly change and take care of my business. I wash my hands when I'm done then brush my hair and teeth. When I'm finished, I take my dirty clothes and head back to my room.

I make my bed quickly and grab my bag with all my textbooks and my notepad inside. My phone shows the time is 9:22 am. I am a couple minutes early so I decide to meet Harley at her dorm building instead of mine. It is closer to the class buildings anyway. There is no need for Harley to meet me at my dorm when it is out of the way for her.

As soon as I reach Harley's dorm building, she is just walking outside. Her dark brown hair is done in a low bun with a few strands falling out. I was too lazy to do anything nice with my hair so I put it half up, half down. Harley sees me and starts walking my way. As she gets closer, I notice she is wearing some light makeup when I decided not to put any on today.

Harley comes up from behind me and loops her arm through mine. "Who's ready to learn about the history of how our world came to be?" she says in a sarcastic tone.

I laugh a little and say, "I doubt we'll learn much today. It will most likely be just introducing stuff probably."

"That's good because my brain is not in the mood for learning right now. It's too early for this."

Harley isn't much of a morning person. Whenever we would have sleepovers, I would be up hours before her. I am feeling tired and a little nervous at the same time if I'm really honest with myself. But I know everything will be fine.

EVERYTHING WASN'T FINE. Harley and I eat a quick breakfast before we rush to the campus class buildings. When we get to our class, there are some seats near the back on the right. There are long brown wooden desks that are separated by the stair aisle leading up to each row. They all face the front of the room where the professor's desk sits. We walk to the back of the room and Harley takes the seat closest to the window while I take the one next to her. The professor hasn't arrived to class yet, it is still a little early.

"Blue?" a voice says.

Jupiter is standing in the doorway. I guess my hopes came true and I will get to see him more often. I give him a smile and wave him over so Jupiter walks across the room towards us. He takes the seat in front of Harley, which is also by the window.

"Harley, this is Jupiter. Jupiter, this is my friend Harley," I say.

Jupiter extends his hand out for Harley to shake. "It is nice to meet you," Jupiter tells Harley while giving her one of his cheery smiles.

"It is nice to meet you too," Harley replies, giving him a smile of her own.

Harley and Jupiter get into a conversation that I don't pay much attention to. Instead, I have my phone out and I text my parents telling them good morning and that I'm getting ready for class to start. I can see out of my peripheral vision that a couple of people take the seats to my right. Suddenly, it is like the sun is blocked from my view. It seems to have gotten darker in the room. I realize everyone is quiet. When I look up, the room isn't dark, it is someone blocking the sun from me. But it is not just anyone standing in front of me.

It's Asher King, and he looks pissed. Just great.

He is wearing a red uniform, meaning his sign is Aries. He is looking down at me with his dark hazel eyes. His stare is so intense, it makes me shudder. What's stuck up his ass? This isn't the Asher I've seen around campus.

I decide to give him a nice cheerful smile, just because I feel like it. "Is there something I can help you with?" I ask.

"Yeah actually, you're in my seat so I need you to move," he says sternly, not returning my smile.

This makes my smile turn to a frown. "Excuse me?" I cross my arms in front of me and lean back in my chair.

"Can you not hear? I said that you need to find another seat," he says, getting even more upset. "This is going to be my seat."

"Are we in elementary school or something? I don't remember seeing a name tag on this seat," I mock him.

I see him clench and unclench his fist. "Listen here, I have already had a rough morning, I don't need you making it any worse. You are going to get the hell out of this seat and find another one. I will sit here and be next to my friends." He motions to my right with his hand.

I look to my right to see who he is talking about. The guy closest to me has tossed hair like Asher's, but his is much darker, like black. My eyes catch his ocean blue ones, I could almost get lost in them. He isn't smiling, he just has a neutral expression on his face, almost like he is bored. This probably happens a lot, that or he doesn't show much emotion. His uniform tells me he is a Virgo.

The guy next to him has short messy ginger hair that still falls down to his forehead a bit. He has a strong jawline and pretty green eyes. I can see he is more fit than the others because I can see his muscles through his shirt and damn. He isn't a super buff type of person but you can tell he works out. He also has light freckles that cover his cheeks and nose. He is the same sign as Asher, Aries.

I look back to Asher and find him still staring at me. What is wrong with this dude? It feels like he is staring straight into my soul and I hate it.

"I don't know if you noticed but I'm also sitting with my friends." I motion to Harley and Jupiter.

Asher looks to see who I'm talking about. When his eyes catch Harley's, she gives him a big smile and waves.

"Don't be so dramatic. You can go and find another seat. Blue and I got here before you. I bet you have other friends in here," Harley remarks while waving him off.

Asher is about to say something, but he gets interrupted by the professor walking into the room.

"Hello ladies and gentlemen. Let's all take our seats and begin. I am Mr. Tidwell, I'm excited to have you all this year." Mr. Tidwell walks to his seat and starts unpacking his things.

Asher says something under his breath that I can't hear and walks away. I look over at Harley and she rolls her eyes.

"You know, I never thought he was the kind of guy that can be a jerk, or an asshole more like it, but I mean, you can't always believe what you see on the internet," Harley whispers.

"I think you handled that perfectly," Jupiter whispers while giving me a wink.

I quietly laugh and turn my attention back to Mr. Tidwell. I may seem fine on the outside, but on the inside, my heart is beating so fast and loud I am surprised no one can hear it. I normally don't talk to people like that, I don't know what came over me or why it happened with Asher, even though he was being a jerk with an attitude.

During one point in class I look over at Asher. It's almost like he can sense me watching him because he looks my way and glares at me. This is just great, now Asher probably hates me even though I didn't do anything to him, he was the one being rude. He may be used to getting what he wants all the time and girls falling all over him, but I won't-

"Alright class, I am handing out this assignment. It has different questions asking about you, your life and it's a way for me to get to know you. All you have to do tonight is answer them and hand them back in tomorrow. Does that all make sense?" Mr. Tidwell asks.

Everyone nods their heads. "Great. For the rest of the time remaining, I am going to introduce something about myself to you."

Mr. Tidwell talks about his family. He has two daughters, Sarah and Jay, who are younger than us. He has a beautiful wife named Carry. He basically talks about things like that for the rest of the time. He and his family live in Tanra, the farmland state. But during the school year he comes to Umbra University and stays in the professors building. It must be hard staying away from your family for so long, but I guess it's the same for me when I'm here.

Mr. Tidwell lets us out five minutes early and honestly, I was kind of glad. I was getting a bit bored listening to him talk the whole time. Walking out I do my best to avoid Asher. It doesn't seem like a problem though because he seems to be avoiding me. Not that I mind.

It is already 9:50 am by the time we get out of history. Harley and I walk together to our next class. Since we got let out early I have about ten minutes until biology starts.

"I'll see you at training," I tell Harley when she walks into her next class.

She waves goodbye then I head down the hall.

HARLEY AND I MEET UP to go to the training facility for class. The training facility is inside a big warehouse. When we walk inside, we can see that the side walls are lined with racks of weapons like knives, swords, daggers, bows and arrows with red and white targets lining the back wall. There are even a few white outlined circles on the floor scattered around the room, so I assume they must be fighting rings. Adjacent to the rings are what looks like fighting dummies. It overwhelms my senses seeing all the equipment and thinking about what's to come in this class.

It seems like most of the people in this class have already arrived. As my eyes search the room, I don't see anyone I recognize. But as I scan the far-right side of the room, I spot Asher and his two other friends from this morning. This is just perfect.

I must have a grumpy look on my face that Harley notices because she asks, "What's wrong?"

"He is what's wrong." Harley looks over in the direction I'm gesturing at. Out of everyone at Umbra University, I had to be stuck with Asher in yet another class. We've already had a rough start, I don't need things to get worse.

Harley rolls her eyes and looks back at me. My gaze moves away from Asher and back to Harley. "Just ignore him. There is no need to get worked up over a guy like him. Besides he said he was having a bad morning so maybe he's fine now."

"You're probably right."

"Hey guys," I tense as the voice sounds like it is close behind me. Looking over my shoulder I find Jupiter standing there. "Did I scare you?" he asks, laughing.

"Oh be quiet." I give Jupiter a little shove, surprised to have another class with him.

A tall man, who looks to be in his forties, walks through the warehouse entrance. He is wearing a black short sleeve shirt with gray sweatpants. His dark brown hair is smoothed back. You can barely see the beard that is starting to grow.

"Hello everybody. I am Mr. Watson, your training professor for the year." Mr. Watson pushes through the crowd of students so he can stand in front of us. Looking at the clipboard in his hand he says, "I am going to start off with attendance. You know the drill, say here when your name is called. Got it?"

Everyone mumbles a yes. "Alright. Floyd Ahmed?"

"Here."

"Bryan Aldred?"

"Here."

Mr. Watson keeps calling out names from his clipboard. He moves his finger down the paper with the list of names, keeping track of who he calls.

"Maverick Everton?"

"Here. You can call me Mav," When I look to see who the voice came from, I find that it is one of Asher's friends, the red head.

"Jules Finlay?"

"Here," The girl who responded has pretty dark colored skin and long curly black hair. Her face is sharp and she looks alert. I wonder if she is always like that.

He keeps moving through the list. He calls Asher's name, then Jupiter's.

"Blue Layton?"

"Here," I call out.

Either it is the sound of my voice or just my name, but Asher looks back at me with a surprised look, but it fades away quickly. He must not have realized I was in this class. Then, instead of frowning at me, he actually grins, like a devilish looking grin. What in the world? I quickly turn away, afraid that if I don't, his grin would just get wider. What is wrong with him? One minute he's all pissed off and now he's all smirks. Mr. Watson calls Harley's name. Later I find out that Asher's other friend is named Dylan Pallet.

"Basically, today we aren't doing any training. I am just going to be introducing things to you and showing you around," Mr. Watson tells everybody. Some of the students sigh in disappointment. "Don't worry everyone, we'll get started as soon as possible. Now if you will follow me over here..." Mr. Watson starts walking towards a rack full of swords and knives.

Everyone huddles around Mr. Watson while he explains the various types of equipment. I feel a little uneasy and look to my right to find Asher standing next to me. His dark hazel eyes are looking directly into my brown ones. I can't be the first to back down so I continue to look at him, with a sudden sense of deja vu. He doesn't seem tense or angry. He just seems...calm. I can't figure this guy out.

I notice I am lost in Asher's gaze because suddenly Mr. Watson's voice brings me back to reality. I realize the same probably happened to Asher because he shakes his head then looks away.

I move my attention back to Mr. Watson, trying to catch up on what I missed. I don't know how much time passed while I was looking at Asher. It felt like a long time, but in reality, it was probably less than a minute. What's up with all these staring contests?

Training class finally ends. Harley and I walk together back to our dorms and the walk to the Capricorn dorm isn't long. I say goodbye to Harley as she walks into the building, then head to my dorm to get any homework I have done.

Later that night Harley and I decide to eat dinner together. We talk about things that happen throughout the day for the classes when we are not together. I briefly mention the situation with Asher. If things are going to be like this with him the whole time, then it is going to be one long year.

After dinner Harley and I go our separate ways. Harley told me there was a party at the Cancer dorms tonight and she invited me, but honestly, I am exhausted and don't even know why considering I didn't do much today. So, I decline her offer and head back to my dorm. I have no doubt Asher and his friends will be at the party, they just seem like those types of people. I have no interest in seeing them again, especially Asher.

Before I fall asleep, I text my parents goodnight. They ask about my first day but since I'm so tired I suggest I'll call them tomorrow. Luna isn't here so I'm guessing she's at the Cancer party, which is fine by me. I kind of enjoy the silence.

# Chapter 6

My first week at Umbra University goes by fast, not much has changed. I still sit in the back by Jupiter and Harley in history class. Asher doesn't seem too happy about that. He will give me dirty looks in class sometimes, but he'll get over it. He got someone to trade seats with him during this past week, so now he is closer to Dylan and Mav. He can be so confusing sometimes because one day he'll give me an annoyed look then the next day I catch him smirking at me. It doesn't make any sense to me, does he hate me or not? But it's not like I care what he thinks anyway. In training class, we are still being introduced to things and going over safety rules. As Mr. Watson likes to say, safety before skill.

This morning is the same as usual. I start my day by waking up at 9:00 am and getting ready for my classes. For my uniform today, the base color of my skirt is brown, but it has stripes that are different shades of brown on top. I never had uniforms in high school so I was worried about how the uniforms here would look, but they turned out better than I thought.

After I'm done getting ready, I meet Harley outside her dorm building. I also invited Jupiter to start meeting us here. Once we are all together, we head to get a quick breakfast at the Corner Cafe.

"Have you seen the news?" Harley asks us as we arrive. I notice she has a worried expression on her face, and has since this morning, possibly because it has something to do with the news she's talking about.

After we got ourselves a table to sit at, a waiter came up and took our orders. We chose a table in the far back corner of the restaurant so I look at all the people eating around us. I notice they seem to be feeling the same way as Harley.

"No," I answer. I never really look at the news if I'm honest. Not that it is not important, it just never interested me much. When there are big events happening, I may check it out, but I should probably start paying more attention just to know what's going on around me.

"I haven't looked at it yet," Jupiter replies. "Why?"

Harley quickly pulls out her phone from her back pocket. While scrolling through her phone she says, "A student at the university died last night at the Leo dorm. It, uh-it says it was no accident."

"So it was a murder?!" Jupiter says a bit too loudly. Some people turn around to look at us.

"Keep your voice down!" Harley whispers. "Yes, it was a murder. And per this article, so far the investigation has shown no evidence of what caused it, or whom. Only that the victim's roommate said they woke to find a dark figure jumping out of their dorm window. At first he thought it was his roommate, but he soon realized he was dead in the bed next to him. Look, it's all here." Harley hands her phone over for us to look at.

Sure enough, a guy named Austin Cohen was murdered in the boys' Leo dorm building just last night. There was no evidence of who did it other than the person looked like a dark figure like Harley said. That means it could be just about anyone. The article says the guards are doing all they can to figure out who it was and make sure they are punished for their crime. They better hurry because I don't like the thought of a murderer wandering around campus.

"That's um-that's scary," I say. I'm honestly shocked to hear about this. I feel growing up I never heard anything but stories about Umbra University being one of the safest places to be with the wall surrounding campus and all the guards. I'm thinking the murderer must have disguised themselves as a student in order to get into campus.

"It's terrifying! I mean, I was out partying while someone was getting god damn killed in their sleep!" Harley shrieks. She puts her head in her hands while her elbows rest on the table and takes a few deep breaths to calm herself.

"It says the guards are doing everything they can. It is shocking, yes, but they will make sure it doesn't happen again. We have some of the best guards at Umbra, the murderer will be found and then we can put this all behind us," Jupiter comments while handing Harley her phone back. She sits back in her seat and takes her phone from him.

We quickly eat our breakfast and head to class without saying another word to each other. We are all still silent on the way to class, too shocked to speak. I never expected something like this to happen, especially here at Umbra University. I just imagined this to be a safe place with all the guards, not to mention the wall. All the University staff even said we would be safe during any orientation meetings or RA introductions, but here we are, trying to process that an intruder got through the wall. As we walk to class, I notice there are more guards than usual patrolling the area.

When we walk into class everyone is already in their seats. Walking towards the back I can hear everybody whispering about what happened last night. Some people even look pale. I don't blame them, it could have been any of us. I'm terrified that it happened on campus, so I can't imagine how Jupiter feels knowing it was so close to *his* dorm.

I take my seat next to Harley and stay silent. As soon as I sit down, I feel my phone buzzing. I take it out and see it's my parents. I assume they have probably heard the news and are checking in on me.

**Mom: Are you alright sweetie? We heard about what happened. We just wanted to check in on you.**

**Me: Yeah, I'm fine. Just a little spooked.**

**Dad: You can call us anytime, okay? If you ever need to talk to someone we'll always listen.**

**Me: I know, I'll call you later.**

Mr. Watson walks into the classroom. He appears calm, he doesn't seem pale like how most students look. Maybe he hasn't seen or heard the news yet? How could he not know though, doesn't the University need to keep all staff informed of something as significant as this? He has to know and is just trying to keep calm so no one starts freaking out.

**Me: I have to go, class is starting. Love you. Tell Emily I said hi.**

**Mom: I will. Stay safe. Tell Harley she can call us if she needs anything or wants to talk.**

**Me: Will do.**

I quickly put my phone away and told Harley what my mom said. I look back up at Mr. Watson and he looks at us with a serious expression, confirming for me that he knows.

"I am sure by now you all have heard what happened last night. If not from the news, then from all the whispers going around," Mr. Watson tells the class. "We know this scares you, it has given us adults a scare too. But please know you are safe here, the number of guards is rising so no one will be able to get it now without permission. If you feel like you are not safe to stay here just let any staff know and we will do everything we can to take additional steps to make you feel safe. Now, we will continue class where we left off. Would you please all open your textbooks to page 187?"

I pull my textbook out and open it to the right page. Mr. Watson reads the text out loud, but I'm not listening. I'm too focused on what happened to be able to pay attention right now. How am I supposed to feel safe when someone has just been murdered? I look around and it seems that others in the class are struggling like me.

I MAKE IT THROUGH ALL my classes...barely. I was too consumed by what happened to Austin to even think straight sometimes. Occasionally I would walk right past my classroom, then have to turn around and backtrack. That wouldn't have been that bad except for the fact that Asher watched me do it one time! God, I'm so freaking embarrassed. I mean out of all people, why was *he* the one who happened to see it? Thank goodness he didn't make any rude comments. It would just make my day ten times worse if he did.

Throughout the day my head has been aching, I'm not even sure why, but now it is pounding and makes it hard for me to focus. Throughout training class I kept rubbing my head, but it's not like that helps anything.

"You okay?" Harley asks me. We are walking back to our dorms now, but honestly, I really don't want to go there. I don't feel completely safe in my dorm anymore and it reminds me of Austin being killed in his. I put on a smile that I know doesn't match my eyes, and Harley can tell. "Oh yeah. I just have a headache, that's all."

Harley is about to say something when she gets interrupted from someone behind me. "You should go to the healing center if your head hurts that bad. I saw you rubbing it the whole class." I turned around to find Asher standing behind me with Mav and Dylan. Perfect.

"Stalking much?" I ask him in a sarcastic tone.

"I am coming from the training facility like you and our dorm buildings are in the same direction," he replies as a lame excuse. If he was eavesdropping, he should just own it. Wait, if he knows that I was rubbing my head the whole time during class that means he was watching me. Why the hell was he doing that?

I turn back around and continue walking. "I'm fine. I don't need to go. I don't even understand why you care." Harley continues to walk beside me. My head feels like someone is pounding their fist against it and unconsciously I start to rub my head again.

"Normally I wouldn't agree with the guy," Harley says looking back at Asher. "But I think we should go so you can get some medicine."

I stop again and turn to face Harley. She has a look of concern on her face. "Just act like he's not here," Harley says, waving her hand in Asher's direction. His face scrunches as Harley's hand almost whacks him in the face. "Instead, you are just taking the suggestion from me."

I think about it for a bit. "Fine," I reply, looking over to find Asher and his friends still here. I realize he not only did he not leave, but he also hasn't answered my question about why he cares. His eyes lock with mine and I quickly look away. I'm just not in the mood to drown in his beautiful, dreamy eyes. Seriously? What am I even thinking? My head must really be messed up if I just called his eyes dreamy.

Harley and I head in the direction of the healing center, which is by the park. As we pass the Aries boys dorm building, I look back to make sure Asher doesn't follow us. Instead of following us, I see him give me one of his shitty grins then head inside his dorm building. My face heats up and I can feel that I am blushing. Why, out of all people, did Asher have this effect on me. I am so annoyed he can get under my skin like this.

"Um, Blue? Your face is turning a little red," Harley states. "Are you feeling worse?"

"Lets just quickly get to the healing center," I reply while picking up my pace.

ONE OF THE NURSES CHECKS my temperature and asks me a series of questions. Like, "On a scale of one to ten how bad does your head hurt?" and other things like that. They end up giving me some Advil to take and send me on my way.

On the way out I ask Harley, "Do you want to do something? Like walk around the park or check out the restaurants here?"

Harley thinks about it for a bit. "Let's go for a walk."

We head to the park which is close by. For the first few minutes, we don't say anything to each other. My headache has already started to feel better and I can't help but think about how Austin's roommate must feel right now. If I woke up to find my roommate dead I would be absolutely terrified right now. I can't imagine what he is going through, or any of Austin's friends and family for that matter.

"How is your family doing?" Harley asks me.

"They're doing good. I think they are a bit shaken by what happened of course, but otherwise, they are doing fine, just worried about us. How about your family?"

"Same as usual. My parents just checked up on me this morning. My dad is still working a lot so I haven't gotten to talk to him much. Mom says they are both doing just fine though." Harley's dad tends to work a lot. He would often miss out on some pretty important events that Harley participated in because of his work.

"That's good to hear, the part about them doing well."

We end up walking around the park, talking about random things, for just over an hour. Eventually we had to go back to our dorms, even if we didn't want to. Once I'm in my dorm I make sure the window is locked, even though it is still light out. I don't want to risk anyone getting in here no matter what part of the day it is. While I'm working on my homework, I get a text from Jupiter asking about eating dinner together. I think to myself that I'm glad we exchanged phone numbers last week. I'm excited at the possibility that Jupiter and I'll become great friends.

I respond telling him I'm just going to get take out and eat at my dorm. Not wanting to walk by myself to get my food, I ask if he'd like to order his own meal and pick it up with me, which he gladly accepts. I haven't seen him too much today other than my first class this morning and again at training class so it will be nice to catch up with him and to be honest, not be alone.

I walk to Jupiter's dorm and meet him there. The walk to the town is nice and we talk more about Jupiter's home life. He tells me about his sisters who seem like great people.

We decided to get food from the Zodiac Grill again. Once inside, we give one of the staff our order and pay. They tell us that we can sit and wait on the benches by the entrance, and it smells so good here, I can't wait to eat.

The door to the grill opens, and as I look up, I see Asher walk through the door. He doesn't seem to notice me as he walks in, thank God. I don't want to deal with him anymore than I have to in a day. Dylan walks in with him, I wonder where Mav is? They walk up to one of the staff and Asher says something I can't hear. The staff member then points in our direction, they must be getting take-out also. Asher turns around and that's when he notices me and grins.

I quickly look away and start talking to Jupiter. "Do you have any pets at home?" Hopefully if I look busy Asher won't talk to me.

"I used to have a dog, but she unfortunately passed away," Jupiter replies. I feel someone sitting in the spot beside me and I bet I can guess who it is without even looking.

"I'm so sorry, if I knew, I wouldn't have brought it up," I replied. The person next to me moves a bit, reminding me that Asher is sitting right next to me. Out of all the spots, of course he chose to sit next to me.

"No need to apologize. There's no way you could have known, it's fine," Jupiter states. "I just really miss her," he says with a sad look in his eyes.

I nod my head in understanding and we go back to sitting in silence again. Out of my peripheral vision I see Asher looking at me. I can feel my face suddenly start to heat up. Is he trying to make me feel uncomfortable?

"Funny running into you here, Blue." I look over and what do you know, Asher has that stupid cocky grin of his.

"I don't find it funny," I mumble. Asher must have heard because his grin turns into a bigger smile.

I look straight forward, but I can feel Asher still watching me. Why does he even do that? I keep catching him watching me like a hawk and it gives me the creeps. What if he's the murderer and that's why I get on edge when he's around? No, it can't be him, I reassure myself.

"Blue," A lady behind the counter says while holding a bag of food in her hand.

Jupiter and I get up from the bench and head over to her. She smiles and hands me the bag of my food. We both thank her and head back outside.

"See you tomorrow," Asher says once we almost reach the door.

"See you tomorrow," I mumble back.

Once we get outside, I look over to see Jupiter giving me a weird look.

"What?" I ask him.

"What was that all about?" Jupiter asks.

"We just-we aren't on best terms," I answer. Jupiter gives me a look that says, explain more. I sigh and say, "He is just a stuck-up guy who I don't want to waste my energy on."

"Hm, I see," Jupiter looks forward and we continue to walk. Why did he say it like that? Does he think something else is going on?

We continue to walk in silence for a couple more minutes, but I get to the point where I can't stand it anymore.

"He just gets on my nerves! He has ever since that first day in history," I blurt out.

"Do you know why he gets on your nerves?" Jupiter asks.

"Yeah, because he seems okay one moment but then acts like a jerk the next! I feel like you're acting like you're my therapist right now," I state. "Which, I guess I'm not really complaining."

"By just asking you a few questions?"

"Yes," I answered. I look over at Jupiter and he is looking at me funny. "No, you aren't. I just felt like you were acting like one. You know what, let's just change the subject."

Jupiter laughs at that and I playfully shove him with my shoulder.

"Hey, watch it! I am carrying your food," Jupiter states.

I was about to shove him again but then stopped, realizing what he said and not wanting my food to get dropped or smashed. We talk and laugh the rest of the way to Jupiter's apartment. Jupiter can always seem to make me smile and laugh no matter what. That's one of the many things I like about him. When we make it to his dorm, he takes his food out of the bag and hands the rest to me. We say goodbye and part ways. Jupiter forgot about the homework he had to do tonight so we decided to get the food together, but eat at our own dorms.

On my way back to my dorm, my mind wanders to last night's events. I can't get it out of my head and it is driving me crazy. Hanging out with Jupiter did help distract me for a bit, which I'm grateful for. Once I'm back in my dorm room, I sit on my bed and spread out my food. While I'm eating it starts to rain. I love the rain. It has always seemed to calm me, it just seems so peaceful and takes my mind off the murder.

After I am finished eating, I throw whatever is left in the little garbage bin we have placed in the corner. When I head back to my bed, I hear the door open. I quickly turn around and see Luna walk through the door.

I must have a frightened look on my face because she asks, "Are you okay?"

"Yeah, sorry. I'm fine." I go back to laying on my bed and pull out my book. Luna and I are both sitting on our beds and it looks like she's doing some homework. As it starts to get dark, I stand up and check the window again to make sure it is locked. I don't want anyone getting in here tonight.

"Thank you," Luna suddenly says.

I look at her confused. She is still looking down at her textbook so I ask, "For what?"

"For checking the window. I was going to do it, but you did, so I wanted to thank you," Luna says looking up at me.

"Oh uh, no problem. Do you plan on going out somewhere tonight?" I ask.

"No, why?"

"I was going to lock the door too, but I wanted to make sure you weren't going out," I responded.

"Oh okay," Luna goes back to looking over her textbook.

I walk over to the door and lock it. Once I am back in bed, I take my book out and start to read again. I'm almost finished with it and think to myself that I'm grateful I brought more than one.

After finishing my book, I switch to reading over my textbooks, but decide I should probably go to bed. It's 9:30 pm and already dark so I get under the covers and turn my lamp off while telling Luna goodnight. I turn so I'm facing the wall because Luna still has her lamp on. I don't blame her because a part of me feels like keeping mine on too, but I know I won't get any sleep with it on. If I'm honest, I might not even sleep with it off.

I don't know how long I lay there. It feels like hours. At times, I almost fall asleep, but I jolt awake at the slightest of sounds. This is going to be a long night.

# Chapter 7

Another week has gone by. Everyone still seems a bit uneasy by Austin's death. But now, I am finally able to get some better sleep. The first few nights after the murder, I wasn't able to sleep. I could not turn my thoughts off and just kept replaying the stories we were hearing around campus about what happened. I would swear I heard something or would startle at the smallest noise. It was exhausting.

I roll out of bed and quickly get changed for class. I'm glad I only have two classes today, history and training. As is our routine, I meet up with Harley and Jupiter, then we head to class together.

I am a bit surprised to see Asher already in his seat when we enter the classroom. He usually comes running in at the last second, so being not just on time, but a little early to class is out of character for him. As Mr. Tidwell walks in everyone takes their seat.

Mr. Tidwell starts his class the same way as usual. He explains the basics of what we are doing today then reminds us there is an exam coming up. Everyone sighs and complains.

"Now, now class, I know exams aren't fun but they are a way to see how much you have learned. Anyways, if you open your textbooks to page-" Mr. Tidwell gets interrupted by a knock on the door. Suddenly a woman walks into the room without even waiting for Mr. Tidwell to respond or invite her in.

She has rich black hair that is put up in a tight bun and wears a black suit jacket with a white button up shirt underneath with black slacks to match the jacket. As her sharp hazel eyes scan over all the students her face has a serious expression, showing no emotion.

"Mrs. Mason, nice to see you," Mr. Tidwell says with a smile on his face.

I know Mrs. Mason is the principal, but I have never seen her in person or even talked to her, yet I can tell she takes her job seriously.

"I would like to speak with you out in the hall, please," she says, keeping her expression neutral.

"Of course," Mr. Tidwell turns towards us. "I want you all to read over section ten while I'm gone," With that Mr. Tidwell and Mrs. Mason walk out of the classroom.

I try to focus on the stuff in the textbook, but my mind keeps wandering elsewhere. Like what I'll have for dinner tonight or thinking of how my family is doing. I realize I wasn't even paying attention to what I was reading and have to start over. I hate when that happens.

Eventually, Mr. Tidwell comes back to the classroom and my heart starts to race as I see he looks paler than he did before. His expression is almost like he has seen a ghost. What did Mrs. Mason tell him? He doesn't say anything to the class, but instead just sits at his desk and stares into space. I look over at Harley and try to give her a look asking what is going on. She just shrugs her shoulders and looks back at Mr. Tidwell.

For the rest of class, we just read parts of our textbook. He doesn't say anything as we leave the class. He just sits at his desk, staring at his paperwork. What on earth is going on?

Harley, Jupiter and I walk out together. Harley has only two classes today, like me so we say goodbye to Jupiter as he heads to his next class.

"What do you think Mrs. Mason told Mr. Tidwell?" I ask Harley as we turn to walk to her dorm and hang out until training class starts.

"I have no clue, It could be anything really," She replies. What if it's another murder?

Once we get back to the dorm, we sit on Harley's bed and play some card games. Around lunch time, we text Jupiter to see if he can eat lunch with us and he replies back saying he will meet us at the Zodiac Grill. We both put our shoes on and head out the door.

Harley and I walk in silence on our way to the restaurant. It is actually a comfortable and calming silence, not an awkward one, which feels good after the anxiety of this morning and whatever Mrs. Mason talked to Mr. Tidwell about. Once we reach the Zodiac Grill, we see Jupiter standing outside obviously waiting for us. He smiles as he sees us approaching, but it doesn't meet his eyes. I can tell immediately that something is bothering him.

Harley notices too because she says, "Something's up."

We immediately both quicken our pace. Once we reach Jupiter, I ask, "Is everything alright?"

"I'll explain inside," and with that, he turns and strides purposefully into the Zodiac Grill. That's odd.

We find a table and quickly but silently take our seats. Soon after, a waitress comes to take our orders and the moment she leaves, I look over at Jupiter and see him staring blankly at the table. Jupiter doesn't say anything as we wait for our food. Harley and I try to make small talk with each other and include Jupiter, but he stays silent and it's really starting to freak me out. I don't want to pressure him into saying anything but what if it has something to do with what Mrs. Mason told Mr. Tidwell?

Finally, the waitress comes with our food and we thank her as she leaves. Jupiter takes a deep breath, it was almost like he was coming out of a trance, he pulls out his phone and tells us, "Take a look at this."

When I look at his phone, I see his hand is shaking and has the local news site pulled up. I read the headline, then went into complete shock.

### *Sally Young Murdered at Umbra University*

**Miss Sally Young (19) is a student at Umbra University. She has been living in the girls Virgo dorm building since the start of school this Fall semester. Sources say Miss Sally was out visiting with a**

**friend at another student' dorm late last night. She left the dorm around two in the morning and her roommate reports she never returned that night. They found her body between the Leo and Virgo boys dorm buildings. Sources say that she had no scratches or markings on her person, but a look of horror was frozen on her face. Next of kin have been located and notified. Services will be held to celebrate her young life in the coming days, more details to follow.**

**There are no potential suspects at this time and no evidence on what may have happened. Some are starting to question if this is the same person/suspect who killed Austin Cohen (19) just last week. Umbra University has told us they are taking precautions and supporting all authorities looking at the case. School officials are contacting all parents, notifying them that effective immediately more guards will be stationed throughout the campus. School officials say they are doing everything they can to find the intruder and stop this from happening again. If you have any details or information, please contact University police immediately.**

I looked away from the phone and the article, unable to read another word. This makes me feel sick and I can't eat my food anymore, so I push it away from me. A rush of panic comes over my body as the realization sets in. Another murder? This can't be right, this can't be happening.

"Another murder? Here?" Asks Harley.

"Yeah, just last night. Something isn't right. It says they don't know if it was the same person who killed Austin, but it has to be, don't you think?" Jupiter asks no one in particular "I can't even process that there could be two murderers on campus."

I hold my hands together under the table to keep them from shaking. There was another murder, here at Umbra University, just last night. What if that was me? Or Harley? Or even Jupiter? I thought they said we were safe and it wouldn't happen again?

"Blue?" I turn towards Harley and she is looking at me with a look of concern on her face. Jupiter has the same look on his face as Harley does. They must have asked me a question, but I wasn't listening.

"Sorry. What did you say?"

"Are you feeling okay? You look really pale," Harley puts her hand on my forehead. "Your forehead doesn't feel hot."

"I'm fine. Just anxious, that's all," I reply.

Looking at both Jupiter and Harley, I can see they look a bit pale too. We all know these murders aren't a joke. For all we know it could have been anyone of us that was the victim. We eat whatever we can stomach in silence.

On our way out, we head over to the park because we each only have training left for today. We found a bench to sit at that was facing a field where a group of boys were playing football. Of course, some of them are shirtless which is very distracting. Looking over the players, I spot Asher, and of course he's on the shirtless team along with Dylan and Mav. I'm not going to lie, he looks pretty damn good without his shirt on, all toned and muscular. To the side I hear Harley ask Jupiter if he's played football before.

"Me? No way, I don't play football," Jupiter says while crossing his arms over his chest and leaning against the back of the bench. "It's too brutal for me."

"Well, if you don't play football, what do you play?" Harley asks.

"I play soccer or sometimes basketball, but I mostly ski. Even if you don't count that as a sport, I still count it as exercise."

"Makes sense."

Jupiter sits up a little, uncrossing his arms. "What is that supposed to mean?" He asks.

"Well, you just seem like the type of person who doesn't play such an intense contact sport because you are scared of getting tackled," Harley says in a confident way.

This seems to get at him because he says, "I'm not afraid to get tackled, I just don't like the sport that much."

"Prove it. Prove you're not afraid to get tackled." Harley looks at Jupiter with an evil smile on her face. There is one thing you should know about Harley, she loves it when she gets her way. When she doesn't, I recommend staying away. Far away.

Jupiter looks at her for a few seconds and Harley still has that grin on her face. "Fine," Jupiter gets up and walks towards the guys. I am a little stunned to see him doing this, but you can't really resist when Harley gives you that grin and challenges you like that.

"Why do you want him to play so badly?" I ask.

"Well, it would be a nice distraction to see someone who doesn't play football play with them," Harley gestures to the guys playing football. "And it is funny to see him out of his comfort zone."

I smile at that because I agree, I could use a distraction. When Jupiter walks up to them, I can't make out what they are saying. The guy Jupiter is talking to points in Asher's direction. He must be on their team. The two teams are split up, and Jupiter walks over to the shirtless team.

Jupiter isn't as bad as you would think for not playing football. His team ends up winning, mostly thanks to Mav, Dylan and Asher. At the end of the game Jupiter is talking to Asher and a few others. They must have asked him something because Jupiter points in our direction. They all look over and see us sitting on the bench, including Asher. Our eyes lock and he gives me one of his grand smiles.

After Jupiter is done talking to them, he runs back over to us. His face is beaming.

"That didn't seem so bad," Harley says as Jupiter reaches us.

He puts his shirt back on. "You're right, that was actually kind of fun."

"Well look at that, I knew you could do it," Harley gives him a pat on the back and starts to walk away. Jupiter gives her a look implying that she didn't know that at all.

We both hurry after Harley before she gets too far ahead. As we head back to our dorms, my mind wanders back to the murders. No, I shouldn't think about that. It will only make matters worse.

We say goodbye to Jupiter and he heads into his dorm building. The rest of the walk back to our dorm Harley and I talk about our classes and all the work we have to do. Thank goodness I don't have too much homework today.

When I get back to my dorm, I finish the little homework I have. Luna comes back from one of her classes and we end up playing war with a pile of cards she brought with her. Luna wins round after round while I only win a few. This game is really just a game of luck. After playing quite a few rounds, she heads out to go hangout with other friends. Sometime in the future I hope to get to know her more because she seems like a kind person, but to be honest, I really don't know much about her.

I find busy things to do to make up for the free time I have. I go for a walk, but it's a short one. Thanks to the circumstances from recent events, and even though it is still light out, I really don't want to be walking around alone for a long time.

At some point in the evening, I get a text from my parents checking in to make sure I'm okay and tell me to be aware of my surroundings, which I no doubt will be. Emily texts me telling me she misses me and to be safe. I realize I miss having Emily around all the time. Some of the people I have talked to before say that they get in a lot of fights with their siblings, but Emily and I get along really well. We rarely have any fights which I am grateful for. We just get each other.

When the time comes for training class, I quickly change into the uniform Mr. Watson provided us. We haven't been doing a lot of things in training class, just going over basic techniques like safety, how to hold a knife and sword. He told us we will be getting into more serious training this week so they provided everyone with a new uniform to wear to class. Everyone is wearing black athletic pants with an athletic shirt that is your zodiac color and also has your zodiac symbol on it finished off with black tennis shoes.

I have always enjoyed the thought of learning how to throw a knife. I envisioned I would feel like I was strong and had lots of power. I would feel like the bad-ass assassins I read about in some of my books. I would even take a pencil and twist it around in my hand pretending it is a knife. I get so excited at the realization that I'm finally going to learn how to use a real knife.

After I change and put my hair in a ponytail, I meet Harley and Jupiter outside my dorm. Harley has her hair put up in braids and tied part of her light green shirt in the back with a hair tie.

When walking into the training facility, there are so many different colored shirts it feels a little overwhelming. There are yellow Gemini shirts, orange Leo shirts and dark red Scorpio shirts. Virgos wear dark green while Sagittarius wear purple. Aquarius wear a blue-green shirt, Pisces have dark purple and Cancer wear dark blue. Then Capricorns rock brown, Aries red, and Taurus light green. It's almost like a rainbow with everyone in one room.

Mr. Watson walks in, wearing a similar outfit, but instead, all black. I assume this way we can identify him as the trainer.

"All right class, I am going to take attendance then we will get started," Mr. Watson starts to call out everyone's names. When he calls out Sally Young's name everyone stays completely silent. I didn't even realize she was in this class.

"Sally Young? Is she not here yet?" Mr. Watson asks.

An Aquarius girl raises her hand. "Yes," Mr. Watson says.

"Well Sally is, um, she won't be here for the rest of the year," she announces.

Mr. Watson looks a little confused at first, but then it must click because his face goes pale and he has a sort of shocked look on his face. "Yeah, that's right. Sorry about that."

For the rest of class, we work on self-defense moves. Mr. Watson shows everyone different defense moves then pairs each of us with one of their own zodiac members to practice. He said it's good we learn these techniques in light of recent events, just in case the perpetrator(s) tries to harm someone again. He reassured us it wouldn't, but it's always good to be prepared. With our partners, someone acts as the attacker while the other has to defend themselves. I was paired with a guy named Logan. We switch back and forth between the attacker and victim roles throughout class.

Training class seems to move by quicker today. I realized that it was probably because I enjoyed the class. Once we are done, I head back to my dorm and take a shower. After I'm changed back into my normal uniform, I end up reading more of my book. I already finished my homework so I don't have much to do. I text Jupiter and Harley to see if they want to do anything, but they are both busy. Once Luna gets back, we end up playing cards again.

"Do you want to go eat dinner somewhere?" I ask her, thinking to myself, this would be a good opportunity to get to know her better.

"Sure", she replies and we get our shoes on and head outside.

We end up eating at a place called The Lounge. During dinner I get to know Luna a bit more and find out that she's adopted and her parents are lesbians. She has a younger brother named Michael, or Mike for short, who is also adopted. She loves reading and art but doesn't have time to enjoy them as much because of classes. Her passion is sketching and I remember seeing some doodles on her notebook when she does homework.

We head back to our dorm room before it gets too dark and I show her some of the books I brought with me to the university. During dinner she told me she likes to read also, so I let her borrow the one I've already read since arriving at school. She also shows me a couple she brought with her. For the rest of the night, we keep the conversation going and get to know each other better. It's around twelve when we decide to go to sleep and I find myself being able to fall asleep easily tonight.

# Chapter 8

It's already Sunday night. Nobody has any classes on the weekends, so Harley and I spend most of the day together hanging out. We end up back at my dorm after eating dinner and when we get back Luna is sitting on her bed reading. She must not have too much homework this weekend.

She puts her book down and asks us, "Do you guys want to play crazy eights?" as she takes a deck of cards out from her night stand drawer.

"Sure," I say.

"Why not," Harley replies.

We sit on the floor, our backs against the beds as we play a couple rounds. After Harley wins the third round she gets up and starts doing what she calls her "winners dance". I tug Harley back down and we all start to laugh. Luna shuffles the cards and starts dealing the next round. It's already dark outside so I get up to shut the blinds.

When I look out the window, I see a couple of people running from behind the Sagittarius dorm building. Then that's when I hear it, the screams. People are screaming from the other side of the field.

"Guys, something is happening at the Sagittarius building," I tell the others with a tremor in my voice.

Luna and Harley jump up and come look out the window with me as even more people are running and screaming from their building. They seem to be heading towards our dorm buildings.

"What the hell," Luna whispers.

"Come on," Harley says, taking off out the door.

Luna and I hurry after her. As we run down the hall people are starting to come out of their rooms and do the same. We hurry out the front doors and rush outside. As the figures get closer, I can see that they are a bunch of girls. They must be from the girls' Sagittarius dorm. Boys from the other Capricorn dorm and boys from the Aries dorm start to come outside and I recognize Asher as one of them. A girl starts to run towards us and thankfully she doesn't seem to be hurt in any way.

"Help...us," She begs and stops in front of us and tries to catch her breath.

"What is going on? Are you hurt?" I ask questions tumbling out of me as I try to make sense of what is happening. More people are starting to appear. Some of them with their clothes torn or blood on them. What the hell is happening?

"They are...attacking us. They...just busted into...the dorm building," The girl responds while trying to breathe.

I look up and see that some of the guards are rushing to wherever the people are coming from to try and help. One of the guards yells at us to get inside.

"What dorm building are you from? Can you tell me your name?" Luna asks as we guide her into our dorm building.

"Scorpio. From Scorpio. My name is Tracy," I was wrong, I thought they were coming from the Sagittarius dorms, but it's really the Scorpios.

"Alright Tracy, you are safe now. You can stay with me for now," Luna tells Tracy.

"I am going to help others inside," Harley tells us. She hurries off towards the people running towards us.

"Me too," I hurry off after Harley.

Who could be attacking us right now? How did the attackers get into the university? There are still screams coming from the distance. More guards run in their direction. I run up towards a girl right as she collapses onto the ground.

I kneel down in front of her and realize there is blood all over her clothes. "They took her. They took her," she repeats over and over again.

"Who? Who did they take?" I ask as I take in her bloody state.

"They took Cora. She was right next to me then they just took her!" she wails.

I put a hand on her shoulder and she tenses from my touch. "Can you stand? I need you to stand up, I am going to help you inside," I ask, but the girl stays kneeling on the ground shaking her head. "Can you tell me your name?" I try asking instead.

She is silent for a moment, then says, "Jay."

"Alright Jay, I need you to stand up for me, can you do that?" She nods her head yes then starts to stand up. I put my arm around her waist in case she falls down again. I don't think she is hurt, but it's hard to tell in the dark. She never answered my question of who took Cora, but I doubt she will be able to answer me since she seems to be in shock. Some of the students start to use their firepower to help people see and navigate in the darkness.

Two figures start to run up to me and Jay. What if they're the attackers? My fears become more heightened and I start to try and move Jay in the opposite direction, away from them. She can't seem to run, but I can't leave her here. This can't be happening. The thought of being attacked floods my mind, but then I start to think over all of the things Mr. Watson has taught us in our lessons. It's not much, but it could be useful enough to get us away from them. Then I realize there are two of them and Jay doesn't seem like she can even fight right now, let alone defend herself. Suddenly one of the figures lights a fire in his hand and that's when I see that it's Asher and Dylan.

"Are you guys okay? Are either of you hurt?" Asher asks. All I can do is stare at him as he looks over me checking for any injuries. There is a scream in the distance and they both look in the direction it came from.

"Come on, put her on my back. I'll carry her," Dylan says. I help Jay over to him and onto his back. We then all start running back towards my dorm building.

"Is that your blood or hers?" Asher asks as he runs right beside me.

I didn't even realize I had blood on my clothes. "It isn't mine and I don't know if it's hers. She didn't tell me if she was hurt or not," I responded.

As we run, I spot someone else crawling on the ground. We both see she is holding a hand over her stomach so Asher and I stop while Dylan keeps going with Jay. We help the girl up off the ground and onto Asher's back. Once we make it to my dorm building, we see there are nurses running into the buildings as well. Once we are inside, we hand the girl on Ashers back to one of the nurses and she carries the girl into one of the dorm rooms.

There are people and blood everywhere. I can't seem to think straight. I almost feel a little dizzy. I look at my hands as they start to shake uncontrollably. Someone is in front of me, but I can't make out who it is. They put their hands on my shoulders. It is becoming harder for me to breathe. There is too much blood and all I can hear are the screams.

"Deep breath. Blue, look at me. Breath like I am," I hear a voice in front of me say. My vision finally begins to clear and I see Asher taking a deep breath in. He takes my hands in his and places one on his chest. I feel the rhythm of his breath and I try to copy him. My breathing finally starts to come back to normal and I start to relax.

"You're okay, just breathe," Asher says as he removes my hand from his chest, but continues to hold them and watch me.

I realize I'm okay, I'm not hurt. I take a look around me, hoping to see anyone I recognize. I need to find Harley.

"Harley," I say, but I doubt anyone hears me. People are rushing everywhere. It's overwhelming. "I need to find Harley," I say, loader this time.

"I'll help you." I completely forgot Asher was still here.

"She could be in my dorm room, come on," I say.

I let go of Asher's hands and take the quickest way to my room and don't look back so I don't know if Asher is even following me. Honestly, I don't care if he is, I just need to find Harley. Nurses are putting injured people in various rooms. Most of the people I pass don't seem to be too injured, just frightened or appear to be in shock. I climb the stairs two at a time. If Harley isn't in my dorm room, then I have no clue where she is. Hopefully Luna is in the room too as I realize I have no clue what happened to her after she helped Tracy.

I finally reached my dorm room. The door is closed and I didn't bring a key, I just rushed out of the building to help. I knock on the door and wait anxiously. The door opens and I see Harley on the other side. Before I can even say anything, she gives me a bone crushing hug, almost knocking me over. As I gain my balance, I squeeze her just as hard back and let out a huge sigh of relief realizing I had been holding my breath.

"I got so scared, I didn't know what happened to you. I came back to your dorm room and the door was open and you weren't here. I decided I should just wait here for you," Harley says as tears fill my eyes threatening to spill over as the relief of seeing her standing in my room floods my body.

"Well, it's a good thing you did or else I wouldn't have been able to find you. Do you know where Luna is?" I ask.

Harley stops hugging me and opens the door wider. "I'm here," Luna responds, sitting on her bed.

I released a breath I didn't know I was holding. "Good to know you are both okay."

I go to walk into the room, but then turn around towards Asher and Dylan, whom I suddenly realize are still standing outside the room. Dylan must have followed us up here without me noticing.

"You guys can come in if you want to," I tell them.

"We should actually go looking for Mav," Dylan suggests.

"Okay, thank you for the help," I replied.

"Anytime," Asher says. They both turn and start to run down the hall.

I shut the door and head towards my bed. "What in the world happened out there?" Harley asks.

"From what I heard, the girls in the Scorpio dorm building were attacked. Nobody knew who it was, but it sounds like there was more than one person," Luna says. "I heard the guards talking so that's how I know all of this."

It's a good thing I was sitting because after hearing that, I think my legs would have given out on me. I've already heard this from Tracy but it's worse hearing it confirmed by guards. I hold my hands together to keep them from shaking and feel a wave of panic go through my body. What if the attackers come for my dorm building next? What if they go after Harley's building? No, I need to stop with the what ifs. The guards are taking care of this, they will catch whoever is doing this. Then everything will be fine. Right?

I spent the rest of the night in my dorm room. Harley decides to stay here for the night and I don't blame her. I feel better with her around, knowing she is alright. None of us get any sleep. There is too much noise coming from downstairs and we are just too frightened. We decide to keep the light on while we all lay down. Even if it doesn't help us sleep, none of us want to be in the dark right now. Harley and I curl up in my bed and shockingly, we both fit. This reminds me of the sleepovers we used to have back home.

It's around 2:00 am when the guards come knocking on our door. They tell us that classes will continue as normal then they move on to the next door. I walk back over to the bed and try to fall asleep again, but once I close my eyes, all I can see are the girls running towards us, screams in the background. If I listen closely, I can hear footsteps from the nurses walking up and down the halls throughout the night.

I wish they would have canceled all classes tomorrow. After what we have been through, I think we need the day off, but I guess the administration wants to keep things as "normal" as possible.

My alarm goes off and I jolt awake. I must have fallen asleep, surprisingly. When I look next to me, Harley is still asleep. My arms and legs feel so heavy and I can barely keep my eyes open.

"Harley," I shake her a little. "Harley wake up," I shake her a little harder. She abruptly pops up to a sitting position and I jump back, almost falling off the bed.

"I'm up," she says while yawning. Even when she wakes up, she still looks beautiful. But I know, without even looking in a mirror, that I probably have terrible bed head.

"Class starts soon. I'll get ready then walk with you to your dorm," I say and Harley nods her head, still clearly tired. I grab my things then head out the door to the bathroom.

The first thing I notice is how quiet it is in the hallway, even with people walking around.

It's the same in the bathroom, nobody wants to say a word. I quickly change and do my business, then I put my hair in a fishtail braid. Once I get back to the dorm room, Luna is up. Harley is sitting on my bed looking at her phone.

"Here, you might want to check this out," Harley says while handing me her phone.

It is a news article about what happened last night. It confirms that the Scorpios girls dorm was attacked, but the guards never caught the intruders. I pause at that. If they haven't caught them, then they are probably still here somewhere. I go back to reading where the article tells us that the guards are going to be on high alert and are trying to find them. This doesn't give me comfort because had they been doing their jobs in the first place we wouldn't have been attacked. The students who saw the intruders describe them as dark black figures because since the lights were out, all they could see were the intruders' frames.

The article goes on to explain more about what people saw. People were being grabbed out of nowhere. One minute you were with someone, the next they're gone. The article continued with more details, but I skipped to the end, too freaked out to learn more.

Seven people died last night and three people are still missing. The article states that the victims have what looks like claw scratches on them, they are extremely pale and have a panicked expression frozen on their faces.

I give Harley her phone back. "That makes me sick," I say. I have to sit down on my bed because my legs are starting to feel weak and I look down to see my hands are shaking.

I sit down for a little bit, collecting my thoughts and calming my racing heart. Why are people killing the students? I don't understand. After a few minutes I put my shoes on and grab my bag. Harley and I head out the door, but before we go, I tell Luna bye, but she just sits on her bed, looking off into space. Eventually she shares that her roommates are going to meet her here so she won't walk alone to class which makes me feel better, so we head to Harley's dorm building. Her roommate must have already left because no one is in her room. I wait for Harley to be done getting dressed, then we head to get some breakfast. Instead of sitting down, we eat in silence as we walk to class, throwing away our trash in one of the garbage bins once we arrive.

While walking to class, I notice there are less people outside than normal. Walking into class, I realize there are less people here too, but rationalize to myself that class hasn't started yet, so maybe more will come. Jupiter is already in his seat when we head to sit down.

"Are you guys alright? I heard what happened and got really freaked out that something happened to you, but the guards wouldn't let anyone over in that area so I couldn't check on you. I was going to text or call, but I can't find my phone and don't know any of your phone numbers to be able to use someone else's cell to reach you."

"Physically fine, yes, but mentally, I don't know," Harley replies.

"Tired too," I add. "Very, very tired," I yawn, proving my point as I put my head down on the desk and closed my eyes.

"If I were you, I wouldn't go to sleep yet, class is just starting," says a voice to my right. I open my eyes to find Dylan taking his seat next to me.

I sit back up and fold my arms across my chest. "Well, I might because I barely got any sleep last night. I feel like I'm going to pass out any minute."

"Trust me, I know exactly how you feel," Dylan replies.

Asher observes in his seat while Mav is sitting next to Dylan and he also looks like he's about to fall asleep. "Good thing you found Mav last night," and at the sound of his name, he perks up and looks over.

"We got separated when helping everyone out, but we met back up outside the Aries dorm building eventually," Mav tells me.

At that moment, a man walks into the classroom, goes straight to the desk and sets his stuff down. He then takes a deep breath and looks around the classroom. "Alright everyone, I am Mr. Jacka. Mr. Tidwell is running late so I will be filling in for him. Today is going to be an easy day in light of the events of last night. Some students are choosing to stay in their dorms for fear of coming outside, so we don't want to do too much work and have them fall behind. We understand this has been very upsetting, but didn't want to cancel classes, so I just need you guys to start where you left off in your textbook and read just one chapter. The rest of the time you can talk and relax. It's been a long night for everyone," Mr. Jacka sits down and starts going over attendance.

I finish reading one chapter in my textbook and wait for Harley and Jupiter to finish. Harley closes her textbook and turns to me.

"I've been thinking, I don't think these murders are a coincidence," Harley states.

"Well no duh they aren't a coincidence," a girl in front of me says. She turns around in her seat and I recognize her as the Gemini girl from training class, Jules Finlay. "It hasn't been a coincidence since the second murder."

She has beautiful short black curly hair. The sun reflects off her dark skin making it look like it's shining.

Harley has an annoyed look on her face. "Well anyways, something is going on here and we need to be really careful. Any of us could be their next target."

"I'm not afraid. I can easily defend myself against these murders," Jules says confidently.

"What if they are specifically targeting certain people or there is a pattern?" Jupiter pipes in. I never thought of that as a possibility. What if I'm on the list? Shivers rake my body as goosebumps cover my skin.

"I thought there was a pattern at first since they killed a Leo rather than a Virgo. But the next victim should have been a Libra if they were going in order of signs, but it was Scorpio," Mav tells us.

"Gee thanks, I feel a lot better," Jupiter says annoyed.

"No offense, I mean they didn't stick to a pattern so you're safe, right?!" Mav replies

"All I was trying to say before everyone started piping in was that we need to be careful. Until the guards catch them, anyone of us could be next," Harley states.

"Alright everyone, let's move on from the subject," Mr. Jacka announces. I didn't realize he was listening.

Jules turns back around and everyone goes back to doing their own thing. Harley, Jupiter and I talk about eating dinner together tonight and what we should get.

Mr. Tidwell never showed up by the time class ended. The rest of my classes were all like history, not many big assignments. By afternoon

I meet up with Jupiter and Harley to head to training class. During class, we work on more self-defense moves where we pair up with partners and one person is the intruder while the other is the victim. At one point, I look over and watch Jules. She really proves her point from earlier, she really can defend herself quite well, tossing her partner on the floor or twisting their arm in an awkward way. You can tell she has done this before so I make a mental note not to pair up with her if I can help it.

Once class is finished, I grab my bag and walk over to Harley, who is standing by the training facility entrance. She is talking with Jupiter and Dylan and I wonder where Asher and Mav are?

"I don't know, earth power is pretty sweet. I can make dirt balls and throw them at you. See," Harley holds her hand out and makes a tiny ball of dirt from the ground just outside the training facility. She then moves her arm and the ball goes flying through the air towards Jupiter. It hits him straight in the head.

"What the heck!" Jupiter is gingerly holding his hand to the spot where the ball hit him. "That may be impressive, but earth power can't do this," Jupiter throws his arm out towards Harley as a gust of wind blows at Harley, knocking her off her feet.

"Oh, you're going to regret that," Harley starts to get up, but I quickly step in front of them.

"Alright guys, let's calm down. No need to be getting into a fight right now," I tell them.

"I say let them fight," Asher says as he and Mav walk up to us. "That would be fun to see," he says, wearing that stupid grin on his face again. If I could, I would slap it right off him. Maybe I should slap him. That would definitely make me feel better.

"Lets just go back to the dorms, okay? No need to get in trouble for something ridiculous," Dylan suggested.

"I agree," says Mav, rolling his eyes.

"Fine. A fight won't change the fact that earth power is the best," Harley states.

"Earth power? Are you kidding? Earth power is lame, fire power is the best. You can literally breathe fire out of your mouth if you want to," Asher says. I wish I could wipe that cocky grin off his face.

"Wait really? No way! Can you do it now?" Jupiter asks.

"No, not right now. You can't just do it right away, you have to prep yourself for it."

"Pathetic," Harley whispers. Her arms are crossed over her chest and she is giving Asher an annoyed look.

"What did you just say?" Asher asks with a pissed off look on his face.

Before Harley can respond, someone screams in the distance. Everyone immediately turns their heads in the direction it came from. I look around and realize we are the only ones here. All the other students including Mr. Watson have already left.

We all look at each other. "Come on," Mav says as he takes off running and we all follow after him. Mav is taller than me so it's hard to keep up with him and his long strides. I don't even know why I'm running towards the danger, but maybe with all six of us we could help whoever is in danger.

We ran past the boys' Capricorn dorm and we all kept going, but suddenly Jupiter stopped between the boys and girls Capricorn buildings.

"Holy shit," Jupiter says as his face goes so pale, almost like he has seen a ghost. He starts to back away from whatever he sees.

We all stop running in the direction where we were going and instead approach Jupiter. I look down the dark alley in the direction where Jupiter is staring and I can barely make out a figure laying on the ground. As my eyes adjust to the dark more, I can see that it is a girl. Her mouth is open like she is still screaming, but no sound is coming out. As we slowly approach her body I look into her eyes, but they are black as night.

"Oh my god. Oh my god," Harley repeats over and over again. I am too shocked to even move or say anything. I am rooted in place. The girl's skin looks so pale it's almost as if life was drained from her body.

"S-she's dead," Jupiter stutters.

"Mav, go get a professor, guard, or someone," Asher says. Mav seems to hesitate at first. "Now!" Asher screams, never taking his eyes off the girl. Mav takes off running back towards the training facility.

I can feel my body starting to shake. It starts with my hands, then moves to my arms then legs, then I can feel my whole body shaking. It feels like it's getting harder to breathe. If those murderers just killed someone here just now, that means they can't be that far away. They could be watching us right now. I start backing away from the girl.

"B-back up. Get away," I tell everyone. Everyone looks at me with a confused expression. "The murderer could be around here," I explained. Everyone seems to realize what I am saying because they start to look around.

A couple minutes later, Mav comes running back with Mr. Watson and some guards.

"We need you all to back away please," one of the guards orders us. We all stand back while the guards search the area and examine the scene. They ask us what we saw, but we explain we only heard a scream and came running, but her body laying here is all we saw when we got here.

All voices around me slowly become muffled. I can't seem to focus. I need to sit down somewhere, on a bench or something. I think someone is saying my name, but I can't tell. I finally just collapsed to the ground. I think someone is squatting down in front of me. My vision is starting to get blurry. I can't stop the tears from falling down my face.

"Blue?"

It's like I float back to reality. My vision clears and I hear everything around me. Harley is also sitting down to my right and Mav is talking to her while Asher and Dylan are talking to Mr. Watson. Jupiter, however, is right in front of me, hands on my shoulders.

"Focus on me Blue. Block everything else and just focus on me," Jupiter says. I look at him and try to calm my breathing. In, out, in, out. After a few minutes my breathing goes back to normal. "Good job. Alright, let's try to stand up now," he puts his hands under my shoulders and helps lift me to my feet.

"Thank you," I say.

"It's no big deal. It's a lot right now and honestly, I'm surprised I'm not having a panic attack," Jupiter laughs and that makes me laugh a little too. "There we go, there's that smile of yours."

The guards and staff that have gathered end up keeping us there for another thirty minutes asking questions and making sure we aren't hurt. Once they release us we all agree to take a walk around campus together because as much as we are freaked out, we don't want to go back to our dorms and be alone with our thoughts. We all stayed silent the whole time, but not in an awkward way. We arrived at Asher, Dylan and Mav's dorms where they head inside so Jupiter, Harley and I leave to grab dinner together. I was grateful to have that time with them. After we finished eating, Jupiter went back to his dorm and Harley said she would come to mine where we hung out for a couple more hours before I walked her back to her dorm.

As I'm about to go to bed, I pull out my phone to look at the news. I drop my phone in shock...Mr. Tidwell has been murdered! I start shaking all over as I realize *that* was why he was not in class this morning. Of all the deaths that have happened, I never personally knew any of the victims, but this time, it was my own professor. Even though I didn't know him that well, I still start to feel numb as the panic floods my body. What will happen to his family? It has to be terrible knowing someone you loved has passed away.

I barely got any sleep that night. The next day, during history class, Mr. Jacka fills in for Mr. Tidwell again, but no one says anything about his death, and that's probably for the best.

# Chapter 9

More deaths happened throughout the week so the campus ended up going into lockdown. No one in, no one out, no exceptions. The head of the university is saying until they figure out who is causing these deaths or until they catch the murderers, we will be in lockdown because they don't want to risk the murderers getting off the campus unnoticed and escaping. Who knows how long that is going to be, yet we are still supposed to go to classes. Needless to say, there are some students who have decided to stay in their dorms instead. I don't blame them, I want to stay in my dorm, but I don't want to fall behind. As long as it's light out, I should be okay, although there was the girl we found dead after training class.

Harley, Jupiter and I walk to history together like usual. Mr. Jacka comes in and writes what we are doing today on the chalkboard for our next project. He has officially become our new history professor.

"Alright class, as you can see from the board, you will be working on a project with a partner," Mr. Jacka explains. He starts to go through the details on what the project is about and what we need to do. "Now for your partners."

He must have written the partners down ahead of time because he picks up a piece of paper and starts reading the names from it. He starts going down the list beginning with Jupiter and Mav getting paired together.

"Asher King and Blue Layton," Mr. Jacka announces.

Of course I get paired with Asher. Out of all the people in the room, Asher King is my partner. What are the chances?

After Mr. Jacka finishes listing all the partners, he tells everyone we have the rest of the class period to work on the project. I look over at Asher to see him still in his seat. Well, if he won't make the first move to work together, I guess I will. I walk over to him and sit in the open seat in front of him and turn around to face him, but he doesn't look at me.

I clear my throat and he finally looks up at me, eyes locking with mine. "Yes?"

"I was thinking..." I start to say.

"Oh boy, not good," Asher interrupts me as I look at him with an annoyed expression. He smiles and says, "I'm just joking with you. Please continue."

I stay silent for a moment, studying him. Then I continued, "*I was thinking,* you could come over to my dorm tonight and we can work on the project there," I suggest.

"Alright. We'll figure things out then. Five o'clock," I nod then head back over to my seat. That was easy enough. He should already know where my dorm is from the Scorpio dorm attack.

All my classes went by fast and before I knew it, Asher was knocking at my door. I quickly set down my dinner and went to answer. When I open the door, my eyes meet his and everything stops for a moment, making me forget what he's doing here for a second.

"May I come in?" He asks in a sarcastic tone.

I shake my head and clear my thoughts. "Yeah sorry." That was weird I think to myself as I move out of the way and he walks in, looking around the room. There is not much in here so I don't really know what he is looking at. I take a seat on my bed, sitting with my legs crossed and he sits on Luna's bed. His dark hazel eyes are watching me with such intensity. I get chills down my spine as we sit there in an awkward silence looking at each other.

I can't stand it anymore. "We should probably do the research first, then we make the poster board," I suggest.

"That sounds good." We both pull out our textbooks and start reading. He's not acting as difficult as I thought he would be.

For the next three hours, we read the textbook, take notes, and share our research with each other. While writing down some notes, there's a big bang that comes from downstairs. Asher and I look at the door then at each other. Everything is silent, then suddenly the screams start. We both quickly get up from the beds and stand there looking at the door despite the screams still going on in the background.

"Do you think we should see what's going on?" I ask. My heart is beating so fast I feel like it is going to pound out of my chest.

"I don't know, maybe. The screams sound distant, so maybe we can just take a peek out in the hall, see if it's safe to get out or not," Asher says. I nod my head and we both start towards the door. "Just stay close to me, okay?"

"Okay."

Asher opens the door and we shuffle out into the hall. My heart is beating so loudly now I can barely hear anything else. Suddenly all the lights in the hall go out. I grab onto Asher's arm, not knowing what else to do but despite the anxiety of the situation, I can't help but notice how muscular his arms are. I expected him to shake me off, but instead he says, "It's okay, I'm right here." We just stand there, close to each other.

That's when the screams stop. I hear something that sounds like footsteps. Slow, heavy footsteps.

"Go," Asher whispers.

We both rush back into my dorm room and lock the door. The light to my room is out so the only thing lighting it is the moon shining through the window. All is silent for a moment. We both stand close to each other, breathing heavily. What the hell is happening? It is silent, too silent.

*BANG BANG BANG*

Asher and I both jump back as someone bangs on the door. Holy shit, it feels like they're about to break down the door. They're coming to kill us. This is just perfect, this is how I die and I'm only 19. I didn't get to travel the world or get married. I'm never going to experience adulthood. I am going to freaking die tonight! It is becoming harder and harder to breathe. My whole body is starting to feel weak and become numb. I won't get to tell my family goodbye.

"Asher. Asher, I don't want to die." I say.

Asher stands in front of me and takes my face in his hands, forcing me to look at him. "We are not going to die Blue, okay?" I realize he is waiting for me to respond. I can't seem to form words so I just nod.

The banging on the door is getting louder and harder. We need to get out of here before the door breaks. Other than the door, the window is the only way out. I run over to the window and look outside. We are one story up, on the second floor so we can't jump out the window from here without risking breaking something. I look around the room for something to help us.

"The bed sheets," I say.

Asher looks over at me with a confused look. "What?"

"We should tie the bed sheets together and hang it out the window like a rope, that way we can climb down. We tie the start of it to the bed frame, hopefully that can hold our weight," I explain.

"That could work," Asher looks at me and has a look of hope on his face. "That could actually work! Hurry!" We both rush and pull the sheets off the bed.

I try to ignore the banging on the door, the sound of the door cracking. We don't have much more time left before the door breaks. I try to tie the knots as best I can. Once they are all tied together, we knot it on the leg of the bed frame. Asher opens up the window and tosses the sheets down. From the view up here, it looks like it is long enough. My window is on the front side of the building so I can see the courtyard from here. There are guards running our way. They are yelling at us to climb down.

"You go first. If they come in here, I'll blast them with my fire," Asher tells me. I look up at him then start to climb out the window. We aren't supposed to use our powers in the building, especially fire, but I don't give a crap at the moment.

The bedsheets are holding my weight for now. As I start to climb down, I hear a big bang. I can still see through the window and I watch as the door breaks.

It is like time goes into slow motion. The figure in the door is tall and dark. I can't see them clearly, but I can see their long claws coming from their hands.

"GOOO!" Asher yells.

I panic and start sliding down the sheets. My hands feel like they are on fire. I see a bright light flash above me then Asher starts sliding down the bedsheets. I drop the rest of the way, landing on my feet and falling down. One of the guards is trying to drag me away so Asher can jump down. One of the guards behind us shoots an arrow through my window. I can't tell if it hits or misses the intruder.

Other guards are helping Asher up and away from the building. I stay frozen in shock, watching the guards run into the building. My knees hurt from the fall. One of the guards is trying to haul me to my feet. As soon as I am standing up, I feel unstable. The guards start to let go and I am about to tell them to wait when someone else catches me. They grab onto my waist, keeping me steady. I look up and feel relieved to see it's Asher.

"I told you we wouldn't die tonight. We're safe. We're going to be okay," Asher reassures me. Tears are threatening to fall, but I won't let them. I don't want to look as weak as I feel.

I'm shocked when Asher hugs me, but when he does, I feel safe and I hug him back. That's when the tears fall down my face and I can't stop them. I hold onto Asher tighter to keep from collapsing onto the ground.

The guards keep us outside and far away from the building. They ask us questions about what we saw. I told them that it was a tall black figure and that I couldn't see much. It ends up being twelve by the time they give the all clear. As if this night couldn't get any worse, they never caught the murderers. I might as well say goodbye to a good night's sleep. Nurses come by and check on everyone. All the survivors of tonight's attack are huddled into a group. I only have some bruises and a cut on my knee, nothing too serious. Asher also just has minor injuries.

We get told that we will have to stay the night at the boys Capricorn dorm. While they gather all the Capricorn girls together, they are also gathering anyone who doesn't live at the dorm. Asher and I part ways with a quick goodbye. Once he leaves, I realize that I really am alone now. There are people around me, but I don't know anyone. I don't even know where Luna is. I don't have my phone to text Harley or Jupiter or even my family.

The Capricorn guys end up having to squeeze into multiple rooms so the girls can have their own rooms. They assign me a room with three other girls and make brief introductions, but I still feel awkward. I have to sleep on the floor with a pillow and blanket, not that I mind, because I know I won't be getting much sleep anyway.

LAST NIGHT WAS AWFUL. The room was completely dark and every time I closed my eyes, the events of the attack flashed through my mind. All the girls are woken up at 8:00 am and get told they can go back to the girls dorm. Honestly, I don't know if I even want to go back.

When I'm outside and walking towards the building I see a brown-haired girl arguing with one of the guards. I soon realize that the girl is Harley. She must be trying to get to my dorm building to see me.

I walk up to them, almost tripping on air once because I'm so tired. "Harley?"

At the sound of my voice, she turns her head in my direction. Once she sees me, she goes crashing past the guard and gives me a bone crushing hug. I try my best to hug her back.

"Oh my god, I was so worried! I heard your dorm building was attacked, so when I couldn't get a hold of you, I started freaking out because I didn't know if you were killed or not. I rushed over here as soon as I could but they wouldn't let me in," She pulls back from our hug and looks me in the eye. She has tears running down her face.

I hug her again and tell her, "It's okay, I'm okay. Just a few bruises, that's all,"

We stop hugging and Harley wipes her eyes. It's not every day you see Harley cry so when she does, you know it's serious. "Come on, let's go inside," Harley says.

As we walk into my dorm, I expect to see blood everywhere, on the floors and walls, but instead, everything is clean. It is like nothing even happened. We get to my dorm room and head inside. The first thing I see is Luna sitting on her bed and she bolts up once she sees me.

"Thank goodness you're alright," she says as she walks over to me and gives me a hug. "I'm so sorry I wasn't here. I was spending the night at my friend's dorm. I can't imagine you going through that alone!"

Luna lets go of me and takes a step back. "You have nothing to apologize for. It wasn't like you knew it was going to happen and you are allowed to hang out with your friends. Besides, I wasn't alone, Asher was here working on our project with me."

That is when I take a good look around the room. They put the sheets back on the bed. I totally forgot about the door being broken but looking at it now, it doesn't even look like anything happened to it. They must have replaced the door while I was gone. There are no burn marks on the wall from Asher's fire power either.

"I really appreciate you guys checking in on me, but I should probably get ready for class now." I walk over to my drawer and pick out a new uniform.

"You probably don't have to go to class today if you don't want to," Luna suggested. "You seem exhausted."

I close the drawer and face them both, their faces full of concern. "I think I should try to go, if I can't handle it, then I'll just come back here." I know myself and right now the best thing for me is a distraction. I'm about to walk to the bathroom, but I don't want to go alone. "Um, do one of you mind walking with me to the bathroom?" I ask.

"Sure. Totally," Harley says. She loops her arm through mine and we head out the door.

When we get to the bathroom, Harley waits outside while I go in. I take a quick shower and change into my uniform. I look at myself in the mirror. I have big shadows under my eyes and a small bruise on my face that I don't even know how I got. Looking around the bathroom, I notice all the other girls looking like me.

The exhaustion suddenly hits me.

Once I am done, I meet back up with Harley outside the bathroom door and we head back to my dorm room. When I walk in, Luna gives me another hug then leaves for her first class. I pick up my phone and see a bunch of text from my parents telling me to call them.

I tell Harley that I am going to call my family and she winks at me then heads out the door. I scroll through my phone and dial their number. It takes a few rings. but they finally pick up.

"Hello?"

"Oh my god Blue! It's you! You're okay! It's so great to hear your voice," My mom says breathlessly.

"It's good to hear yours. Listen, I don't have much time before class, but I wanted to hear your voice and let you know I'm ok...did you hear about what happened last night?" I ask her.

"Yes, we were worried sick when we heard what happened," my dad tells me.

"I am tired and a bit frightened, but other than that, I'm fine," I lied. I am actually exhausted and terrified, but I don't want to tell them that.

"Well that's good to hear. We won't keep you long. Make sure to give us a call later, okay? Love you sweet heart," my mom says.

"I will. Love you."

"Love you Blue!" Emily yells from the background.

"Talk to you later," says my dad.

"Bye," I hung up and put my phone in my bag.

I stand up and head to class, meeting Harley in the hallway where she's been waiting for me to finish my call. When I walk into the room, I barely have time to register anything before Jupiter comes running up to me. He gives me a big hug, almost knocking me over.

"You don't know how happy I am to know you are okay and alive," Jupiter tells me.

"I'm pretty happy about that too," I say and that seems to get a laugh out of him. I put on a smile for him even if it isn't real.

I take my seat along with the others. I'm so tired, but I'm honestly too scared to fall asleep. After what seems like thirty minutes, Mr. Jacka walks into the classroom. As usual, he writes the plan for today on the board.

"All you guys are doing for today is working with your partner on your project. So go ahead and get to work," Mr. Jacka announces.

I grab my bag and head over to sit by Asher sitting in the seat in front of him and facing him. I pull out my textbook and try to focus on the words. After a few minutes I put my head down on the textbook.

"You should get some sleep," Asher says.

"Can't, too afraid," I mumble. I look up to find Asher watching me.

He looks around the room then turns back to me whispering, "That thing last night, it wasn't human."

Thinking back on it I realize suddenly that he might be right that whatever attacked us last night wasn't human. I don't know what it was, but I remember it having what appeared to be claws. The panic of the moment made me forget until now. "It was like something from a kids nightmare," I state.

"Yeah and whatever it is, there was more than one. Their victims have only been people on campus, what's up with that?"

"Let's not talk about it anymore, please. Can we just focus on the project," I look back down at the textbook, but I keep reading the same sentence over and over again.

"Alright," he says, sounding like he would rather continue the conversation.

With class going by really slowly, I almost fall asleep, but then the events of last night startle me back awake.

As class ends, I pack up my things, getting ready for my next class. I'm so grateful I only have three today.

"Blue?" I look over at Asher. "Do you want to come over to my dorm building at six? We can work on the project there," he asks.

I hesitate for a second. "Sure, I'll see you then."

"Perfect," I am a little surprised when I see him smile. Like, actually smile. Not that up to no good rotten devil grin he typically gives me.

AS I GET CLOSER TO Asher's dorm building, I can see him waiting outside for me. I quickly ate dinner before this and I tried to take a nap, but I wasn't able to fall asleep.

"Hi," I say, walking up to him.

"Hey. Come on inside, I'm starving," he says while opening the door for me.

The boys' Aries dorm building is the same as every other dorm building except they have posters on the walls saying *"Aries Rules!!!"* or *"I'm an Aries, that's my excuse."* making me laugh...whatever!

Asher's dorm room is on the second story, like mine. He unlocks the door and we walk in. There are football and basketball posters on the wall and he and his roommate have a calendar with cars featured on the far corner wall. I'm surprised to find his room actually clean. There are a few things that can be picked up, but otherwise, it looks nice.

Mav is laying on one of the beds, reading a book. "I didn't know you liked to read," I say.

He looks up at me from his book. "There are a lot of things you don't know about me," he says sarcastically with a wink and goes back to reading.

I take a seat on Asher's bed and start to pull out my things. Asher takes a seat next to me, our legs almost touching.

"There is no need to worry about me bothering you. You won't even know I'm here," Mav says, his eyes never leaving his book.

"Thanks Mav," Asher chuckles a little, while picking up his food. "Have you eaten already?" he asked me.

"Yes, I have," I reply as Asher nods his head then starts writing things down in his notebook.

If I'm being honest, I had fun studying with him and comparing our notes. I wasn't worried about what happened the night before or about the walk back to my dorm. I actually felt relaxed and safe. I must have dozed off at one point because I woke up to Asher slightly shaking my shoulders.

I sit up and stretch my arms out and realize Mav is asleep on the other bed. "What time is it?" I ask.

"Eleven. I'll walk you back." I nod my head and put everything back in my bag then we head out the door. I feel better knowing Asher is with me and that I don't have to walk alone. It's hard to believe that he is actually acting like a gentleman right now.

On the walk back, Asher and I talk a bit about our families. He makes me laugh a couple of times and I find myself smiling, like a genuine smile. It's weird how Asher can have this effect on me now compared to the way he used to get under my skin. After he drops me off at my dorm, I tell him to be safe on his way back.

That night I'm actually able to get some sleep. I do wake up a couple of times feeling anxious and finding myself trying to calm my breathing, but at least it's better than the night before.

# Chapter 10

The past week has been slow and agonizing. The Cancer and Pisces dorms have each been attacked leaving so many people dead in just a week. I feel sick just thinking about it. We've been told to stay in our dorms for the past couple of days as a result but is this really the safest thing considering all the other attacks have happened in dorms? The only time we go outside is when we need to get food. Luna and I decide to stock up on food so we don't have to go out as much. We don't have a mini fridge to keep our perishable food in so we mostly eat peanut butter and jelly sandwiches and soup. I've been keeping in touch with Jupiter and Harley, and though they seem to be doing fine, my anxiety feels overwhelming. My family is worried sick so I call them every day to let them know I'm fine. I've been reading so much because that's all I have to do other than sitting around playing card games with Luna.

The professors were given short notice that classes would be shut down for a few days for security reasons, so before we left class that last time, my professors just told us to read the textbooks to keep up until we could return to class. Mr. Watson gave us easy exercises to do so we would stay fit. I have to make use of what little space I have in the dorm. When I get super bored, I look out the window and watch the leaves blow in the breeze. I find that my favorite days are when it rains, which doesn't happen much. Sometimes I wish I could just go home.

This particular evening Luna and I are eating dinner together, a gourmet meal of peanut butter and jelly sandwiches once again with an apple and some chips, when both of our phones "ding" at the same time. We both look at each other then pick up our phones.

It's an email from Mrs. Mason, the principal. She is making an announcement telling everyone we are supposed to start coming to class again tomorrow, that's all it says. Why are we going to class again with the murderers still out there? I don't even feel comfortable stepping outside knowing I could be killed at any moment. Soon after getting the email, I got a text from Harley.

**Harley: Did you get the email about class?**

**Me: Yeah. They might have caught the murderers and haven't said anything yet.**

Even if that's true, they should have mentioned it in the emails. Why does it feel like they are withholding information from us students?

**Harley: That could be it. But, don't you think they would tell us if they did? It makes no sense. Whatever. I have to go. Talk to you later.**

**Me: Bye, stay safe.**

Something seems off about this. You would think they would have written something on the news about catching the murderers. Maybe they are keeping it a secret, but that doesn't make sense either.

After dinner I read more of my textbook. I'm almost done with it thanks to all the free time I have. Once it is ten, I decide to head to bed. Sleeping at night has gotten better. I am able to fall asleep faster, but I still have nightmares and I sometimes wake up screaming and find Luna trying to comfort me. Fortunately, I don't have them as much anymore.

THIS MORNING, I MET up with Harley outside her dorm. Relieved to see each other, we give each other a big hug, then we head to breakfast. We aren't going to sit down in the restaurant so we just get a to-go order. We cat on the way to class so we aren't late. As we walk, I find myself scanning the surroundings, expecting someone or something to jump out of the shadows.

I didn't realize how much I missed walking to class with Harley or how much I would miss just being outside. It was getting boring being locked up in my dorm. There are a lot more people out today and I smile seeing the campus filled with people, although not as many people as before the attacks. It's no longer as depressing when no one is outside. We meet Jupiter outside the class buildings and we all walk to history together.

By the time class starts, I can tell there are less people than usual. I don't want to guess what that means. I haven't been in contact with Asher, but I'm glad to see him in the classroom.

"It is good to see all your lovely faces again. Before we start any assignments or stuff like that, Mrs. Mason is going to come in and have a little talk with us. While we wait for her, you can all talk among yourselves," Mr. Jacka announces.

Jupiter, Harley and I catch up on things we heard or saw while we wait. At one point, Jules joins in on our conversation.

After talking for a while, someone knocks on the classroom door. Without waiting for an answer, Mrs. Mason walks into the room and I'm caught off guard to see several guards follow after her. This could mean that they haven't caught the murderers.

"Mrs. Mason, good to see you," Mr. Jacka says while having a cheerful smile on his face.

Mrs. Mason doesn't say anything back to Mr. Jacka. She just walks up next to his desk then faces us. The guards all position themselves around her. When looking at Mrs. Mason, I can tell there is something different about her, I just don't know what yet.

"Good morning everyone. It is good to see you all here," Mrs. Mason pauses and looks over everyone, studying them. "You are all probably confused about my message sent yesterday for all to return to class with no further explanation. The board and I have talked and came to the decision that we should send everyone back to class. Though we have not yet detained the individuals behind the recent attacks, we will have guards standing outside every classroom door and outside the class buildings for your safety. Basically, to sum this up, we will have guards everywhere so you guys feel safe and protected."

I realize with a sickening feeling I know what's different about her. Her eyes are pitch black. Black as the night. Her eyes weren't that color before, were they? No, I'm convinced they weren't.

"You all will report to class like normal unless you are told differently. Do you understand?" Everyone mumbles a yes. "Good, that is all," Mrs. Mason walks out of the classroom, guards following behind her. That was weird.

"Thank you, Mrs. Mason," Mr. Jacka says, but Mrs. Mason says nothing back, just walks out of the room. "Well, last time we were in class, we were working on your projects so why don't you all pair up with your partners and get back to work."

This time Asher comes over to me. Jules gets out of her seat and goes somewhere else in the classroom to be with her partner leaving Asher to sit in the empty seat in front of me. He gets his textbook and notebook out and turns to face me.

"Asher?"

He keeps reading the textbook, not looking up at me. "Hmm?"

"Did you see Mrs. Mason's eyes?" At this he looks up at me with a confused expression.

"No. Why?"

"They were black. Like pitch-black. I don't remember them being like that before," I tell him.

"Black? Maybe it was just the way the light was shining," he replies. He goes back to reading, not concerned at all, but something isn't right. How did he not see? Was he even paying attention?

After class I tell Jupiter and Harley the same thing and they tell me they saw it too. At least I'm not going crazy.

"We just need to be cautious about our surroundings," Harley says.

"I know. I just have a bad feeling about all this," I tell them.

AS THE DAYS GO BY, all is silent, no deaths, no screams. Nothing. I feel uneasy about the silence. Mrs. Mason keeps reassuring us that it's because the guards are taking care of things and that everything will be fine. Every time I see her, her eyes are still black leaving me feeling *very* uneasy.

Harley, Jupiter and I are walking to class together the next morning eating our breakfast as we go. We don't like to sit down at restaurants anymore in case of an attack.

"I hate having to wear a skirt all the time. Like, what if I want to wear sweatpants one day? What if I just want to be comfy?" Harley expresses.

"Well you should take that one up with the board, because I feel the same way about the uniform, but at least I don't always have to wear a suit jacket or a sweater over a white shirt like some other schools. It can be so hot outside and then I get all sweaty, but then again, I guess that's comfier than a skirt in your defense," Jupiter claims.

"Brag much," Harley responds, rolling her eyes and starts to walk faster. Someone woke up on the wrong side of the bed today.

We get to class and take our seats, but Mr. Jacka isn't here yet. I sit thinking how I miss having Mr. Tidwell around. He was a nice professor, not too harsh on us. I look over to see Jupiter and Harley in a conversation, too quiet for me to hear, but I'm assuming they are continuing their uniform convo. I personally don't mind the uniforms. I still get to wear whatever I want when I'm back at my dorm and on the weekends, so they don't bother me since we don't have to wear uniforms all the time.

I'm about to pull my book out of my bag when people start screaming in the hallway. The screams sound distant, but they quickly get louder and closer. Everyone is up and out of their seats in an instant. I can see people running down the hall through the little window in the door.

Suddenly a random student runs into our classroom panting and out of breath, slamming the door behind her. She has straight jet-black hair and, based on her dark purple uniform, she is a Pisces.

"We are being attacked! Everyone get out now!" she yells. She immediately locks the door, then we all start rushing towards the windows. Thank goodness we are on the first floor. I quickly hurry over to Jupiter and Harley where I find Jules is also with them.

Everyone is trying to unlock the windows. "They won't open enough for us to get out!" one kid yells with panic in his voice.

Once Jupiter unlocks the window he's standing in front of, we realize they are right. The window won't open big enough for us to get out.

"Everyone get out of the way!" I look behind me to find Asher carrying a chair over his head in our direction. I back away and watch as he throws the chair at the window. Surprisingly, it only takes one throw for the window to shatter. Everyone else starts doing the same thing.

"Go!" I yell at Harley. She hurries out the window, trying to avoid the broken glass. Once she's out she turns back towards us.

"You next," Jupiter says in a surprising calm voice. I have no clue how he's not freaking out right now.

I try my best to quickly climb out the window. Harley helps me as best she can from the other side. I feel my leg get cut on a piece of broken glass, but that is the least of my worries right now. Once I'm out Jupiter quickly climbs out the window Asher broke for us and I can see that the other students are climbing out of the other windows. One of the students I'm watching ends up cutting her leg really bad in her rush to get out and she is bleeding everywhere. Another guy picks her up and takes off towards the dorm buildings. I look back at the window to see Jules climb out swiftly and easily.

"Everyone head towards the dorm buildings!" someone yells.

My heart is pounding so loudly and hard in my chest. I grab Harley's arm and yell, "Come on!" as I take off running towards my dorm building.

I can't see them, but I hear footsteps trailing close behind me and assume it is Jupiter and Jules. All around me students and professors are running everywhere. Out of my peripheral vision I'm relieved to see Asher, Dylan and Mav running the same way we are. I hurry after them and try to catch up. When I almost reach Asher, he looks behind himself suddenly. He must have thought I was one of the murderers because when he realizes it's me, his shoulders relax and he seems to become less tense.

As we run through the class grounds, I finally see them. The intruders. This time, it is broad daylight, so I can see them clearly.

They are not human.

"Holy shit," Jupiter yells.

"What the hell is that?" Jules pants.

"I don't know!" I yell back.

The intruders are tall black figures, well over six feet tall, with some sort of black mist around them. They have no facial features except for the devilish grin they are giving everyone. Their teeth are like sharp blades, ready to tear through anything. Dark saliva drools out of their mouths like they're ready for a snack. As my eyes move down their form, I see it wasn't my imagination, they really do have long black claws.

We all run together, in a little pack. My legs are so tired they start to literally burn and I know the only thing that is keeping me from standing in shock is the adrenaline coursing through my body. People are screaming and collapsing all around me. Are they freaking dead?!? I think I'm going to throw up. Just then I see a figure to the side jump on a running student, knocking them both down. I don't see what happens next as I continue to run but I hear what I assume is the horrified scream from the victim.

We are getting closer and closer to the dorm buildings. We make it to the Aries boys dorm and Asher and Mav yell at us to follow them. We all rush inside and up the stairs, towards their dorm room. How are we all going to fit? There are seven of us I think in a panic to myself, but we will just have to make it work because we don't really have a choice right now.

Asher runs up towards the door, but realizes he doesn't have his key. "Shit!"

"Move, I have one in my pocket," Mav pushes past Asher and frantically unlocks the door as his hands shake violently.

We all rush inside their room. Surprisingly, there is more room than I remembered so we aren't as squeezed together as I initially thought. We all stand there for a while with the only sound in the room being our panting as we try to catch our breath and process what the hell just happened. Finally, Asher moves to sit on his bed and invites the rest of us to get comfortable. All the adrenaline starts to leave my body and the pain in my leg comes back with a vengeance. I look down to find blood running down my leg.

"Um, do you guys have a first-aid kit?" I ask. Everyone can sense something in my voice as they look over at me then at my leg.

"Oh my god Blue!" Harley shrieks.

Asher rushes to his dresser and pulls out a first-aid kit. "Sit," he motions to his bed. I stumble over and carefully sit down, trying not to get any blood on the bed.

Sitting on the edge of his bed, Asher squats in front of me. "Mav, do we have some napkins or paper towels?" he asks.

"Yeah," Mav quickly grabs the paper towels and hands them to Asher.

Everyone just watches in silence as Asher slowly and meticulously wipes the blood off my leg. I wince from the pain and Asher apologizes, pausing to look into my eyes and assess if I'm okay. Then, since the band-aid he picks up he realizes is too small, Asher takes out the roll of gauze and gently wraps it around my leg making sure there is enough pressure to stop the bleeding, but not too much to cause discomfort.

"Didn't take you as the doctor type," I say through gritted teeth trying to think of something other than the pain.

"I mean, you don't have to be a doctor to know how to do that," he answers with a smart aleck tone.

"Well still, you didn't freak out. Most people freak out when they see blood," I respond as Asher stands up and throws the bloody paper towels away. I watch him as he crosses the small room and puts the first-aid kit back in the dresser.

Mav moves to sit down on his bed and gestures for Dylan and Harley to do the same. Asher comes and sits by me again while Jupiter and Jules stay standing. We are all silent for a moment. I still can't believe what just happened, but the cut on my leg proves it. I look over at the window and see that the blinds are open.

I get up from the bed and close them. "Probably better if they're closed," I tell everyone. I stand there for a second, then carefully walk back over to the bed assuming my spot next to Asher thinking to myself that the cut wasn't too deep so I assume it should heal quickly.

After more silence, Jules finally asks, "What the hell were those things?"

Everyone is silent, because none of us have an answer. If it isn't a human then what is it?

"The night I was working with Blue on our project, when the dorm got attacked, I blasted my fire at it and that's when I saw what it looked like. It was the same thing we saw today. It made this horrible ear-piercing scream when it caught on fire and I jumped out the window before it could do anything else, so we at least know they don't like fire," Asher explains. I don't remember hearing the thing scream, but I was probably too focused on getting down the bed sheets safely.

No one says anything back because we don't know what to say. Frankly, we have no idea what is happening other than we were attacked yet again today by some unknown creature. I suddenly want to call my parents just to hear their voices to calm my nerves, but I can't because my phone is still in the classroom where I left it in my panicked rush to escape.

Thirty minutes of silence is intermixed with occasional small talk within the room, but I sit shaking in silence, not knowing what to do with myself.

"How long do you think we are supposed to stay here?" Harley asks.

"Until they tell us we can come out," Jupiter answers. Harley nods her head in understanding.

After about three hours of sitting and standing around, Mrs. Mason makes an announcement over the loudspeakers. I didn't even know they had loudspeakers.

"Hello everyone, this is Mrs. Mason. Do not worry, all the danger has passed. You are free to leave your dorms or wherever you were hiding. Things have been taken care of. Have a nice evening and stay safe." When she finishes talking, everything is silent. Why can't they just let us leave and go home?

"I don't really feel comfortable going outside yet," I confess.

"I feel the same way," Harley says.

"I feel a little uneasy about Mrs. Mason. She just seems to be a bit strange lately. I also don't understand what she meant when she said things have been taken care of? They obviously have not," Jupiter tells everyone.

"I agree," I say.

"There have been a lot of strange things going on. I wouldn't be shocked if something did happen to Mrs. Mason," Dylan says.

"Well, I'm hungry and if Mrs. Mason says we can leave, I need something to eat before I turn into one of those monsters myself," Jules jokes, but nobody seems to find it funny.

"Not funny Jules. Not funny," Jupiter says.

"Shut up," Jules warns.

"Some of us probably should get some food, it's getting close to lunch anyways," Mav comments. "And Mrs. Mason did say we could go outside so we will have to trust her."

"Some of us will go get the food while the others stay here," Asher suggested.

"Alright," Harley says.

"I'll go," Dylan announces.

"I'll go too," says Jupiter.

"Putting on your big boy pants, are ya?" Jules says in a sarcastic tone towards Jupiter.

"You better watch your mouth before I put a sock in it," Jupiter snaps and points his finger in her direction. Jupiter must be getting hungry too because he is in an unusual grumpy mood.

Jules swats her hand at Jupiter's finger. "Get that thing out of my face. I'll go too, I'm not afraid to face those creatures."

"Yeah, sure. We'll see about that," Jupiter mumbles.

"What did you just say?!" Jules growls at him with a scowl on her face.

"Alright guys, let's calm down. No need to get upset with each other. Just quickly get the food and come back," Mav interrupts.

Jupiter, Dylan and Jules put their shoes on and start to head out the door.

"If we aren't back in an hour, we're probably dead," Jupiter says before leaving.

"Jupiter! Don't think that way," I say.

"I'm just saying. If we don't come back in an hour, just assume we are dead and figure something else out," I give him a look that explains how uneasy I feel about this. "Calm down, I bet we'll be alright," Jupiter shuts the door and we are all silent.

I sit on the edge of the bed and wait for them to get back. My leg is bouncing up and down because of how anxious I feel. How long should it take them to get the food? Should more of us or maybe all of us have gone to get the food? I can't seem to keep my leg from bouncing as my thoughts spin around thinking about Jupiter, Dylan and Jules and whether they are ok.

"Why don't we get to know each other a little better. We can just ask each other questions while we wait to take our mind off things. If it is too personal then you can skip. I'll go first. Where are you guys from?" Mav asks.

"We are both from Prusmé," Harley answers. "What about you?"

"Dylan, Asher and I grew up in Gena together," Mav answers.

I've been to Gena a few times and have loved it. It is the forest state, as everyone likes to call it, because of the enormous forest called the Golden Territory Woods that consumes almost the entire state of Gena. A large number of the people from Gena live in these cool unique cabin homes. Whenever I've had the opportunity to go there and see one, I am reminded of how incredibly beautiful they are. Some are in the shape of a triangle with a roof so long it goes all the way down to the ground.

"Gena, nice. Do you guys like to hunt?" Harley asks.

"I do, but not as much as Dylan and Asher," Mav replies. We all look over at Asher, waiting for him to say something.

"I like the feeling of the bow in my hand and watching the arrow fly through the air," Asher says quietly, not quite making eye contact with anyone in the room.

"Hunting seems like a fun thing to try once," Harley says.

"How long have you guys known each other?" Asher asks Harley and me.

"Since we were six. We met back in kindergarten and have been best friends since," I answer. I look over at Harley and give her a smile. She winks and smiles back.

"How about you three. How long have you guys known each other?" I ask.

"Our parents are childhood friends so we've basically known each other our whole lives," Asher says.

"Do you guys have any siblings?" Harley asks.

"I have an older brother named Jack and Dylan's an only child," Mav says.

"Bella's my younger sister and she's eleven," replies Asher. "Do you guys have any siblings?"

"Nope, I'm an only child like Dylan," Harley says.

"I have a younger sister named Emily, she's close to Bella's age," I tell the group.

We keep asking each other questions to distract ourselves while the others are gone. I have to admit, it is nice to get to know them better and after about thirty minutes or so of waiting the others return with food.

No one appears to be hurt, which is a huge relief, but I realize with surprise that a girl I've never met before walks in with Jupiter, Dylan and Jules and none of them acknowledges the newcomer. The girl has straight light blonde hair that falls to her shoulders and stunning pale blue eyes. She has ivory skin and full pink lips, but I can see the area around her eyes is red, she must have been crying.

"Who's this?" Harley asks.

"This is Willow Jackson. When we were getting the food, we found her outside alone. She said she didn't know where any of her friends were so we invited her join us," Jupiter explains. He looks at Willow, but she doesn't say anything and is avoiding making eye contact with any of us.

"It's nice to meet you Willow," I say. She just nods and continues to look at the ground. I can't imagine how she felt being alone out there and my heart hurts for her.

"Well, we got the food so let's eat," Jules says walking in with a bag of food. Dylan follows her into the room with another bag and someone shuts the door.

"You can have some of my food," Jupiter tells Willow.

"Thank you," she mumbles quietly, still keeping her head down avoiding looking at him.

We all dig into our food in silence including Harley and I despite the fact we are splitting a salad.

"Did you see anyone outside?" I ask them.

"There were some people out, but I think they were doing the same thing as us, getting food because they were heading in the same direction," Jupiter says.

"That makes sense," I reply.

When the others were out getting food, they didn't just get things for lunch, they also got some snacks for later. I stand up grabbing the snacks and decide to help find places in the dorm room to put them so they're out of the way as we are somewhat crowded in the room.

We end up spending hours in Asher and Mav's dorm room. We ask each other more questions where I find out Jules is from Bonleno. Bonleno has a bunch of small towns in it as well as factories. My Aunt and Uncle live there so I visit a lot. I can't help the smile that creeps on my face as I think about how much I love walking around and looking at all the little shops when visiting there.

Willow doesn't talk much, but she does share details about how she lives in Tanra and that she loves tending to all the goats on their farm. Tanra is what I like to call the "farmland". It's where most of our nation's food is grown. I have seen beautiful pictures of the flower fields there. I have never been to Tanra, but I want to go one day. It reminds me of the beautiful country sides I read about in my fantasy books.

"What do you think we are supposed to do now?" Harley asks.

"Maybe some of us can go back to my dorm and stay there for the night. That way it's not as crowded. Then tomorrow maybe we can all meet up again?" I suggest.

"That sounds good. All the boys can stay here," Mav says.

Harley and I stand up and put our shoes on. "I think I'll head back to my dorm and see if my friends are there," Jules says.

"Okay, sounds good, but can we walk you to your dorm just to be safe?" I ask her. "You can always come back and join us if you'd like, or in case your friends aren't there."

"I'll be fine. No need to worry about me," she heads out to the hall and shuts the door. She didn't sound as confident when she said that last part.

I look back at everyone else and notice Willow is still sitting. "Do you want to come with us Willow? Or do you want us to bring you to your dorm?" I ask her.

"I'll just go with you guys," she says.

"Okay." We exchange numbers and say our goodbyes then head out the door.

As I go to shut the door, Asher says, "Be careful." I look up at him and his face has a concerned look on it. I didn't know he would be this worried about us.

"We will. I'll text you when we get back safe," I say as I shut the door and we walk down the hall.

LATER THAT NIGHT, NONE of us could sleep. Harley and I shared my bed while Willow had Luna's. Luna never came back to our dorm that night which makes me feel unsettled. I hope she found somewhere else to hide and that she's alright, maybe staying with her friends.

In the morning, Mrs. Mason makes an announcement saying there will be no classes today. I feel relieved because even if there were classes today, I probably wouldn't have gone.

I woke up early in the morning to find Willow already awake. I realize my bag and stuff are still in the classroom we escaped from so I will have to get them sometime soon, but I have no desire to go find them alone. Maybe if the guards are going through the classrooms, they will find a way to give us our stuff back so I don't have to get them myself.

Harley sleeps through Mrs. Mason's announcement so I decide not to wake her up because she didn't get much sleep last night.

A little later there is a knock on the door. I open it to find Asher, Mav, Dylan and Jupiter on the other side. They have a box of donuts with them and I can feel myself relax just seeing them standing at my door.

"Donuts," I say excitedly. "You guys can come in, but be quiet. Harley is asleep."

"Still?" Jupiter asks while walking in.

"None of us got any sleep last night," I tell them.

Willow is sitting on the bed with her back up against the wall. Jupiter walks over and sits next to her putting the box of donuts on the bed between them.

"Tell me about it, I had to sleep on the floor," Jupiter complains while opening the box and taking a donut out.

"Donuts?" Harley jerks awake, scaring everyone in the room. She looks around at everyone in the room. "Why didn't you tell me we had company?" she asks, looking a little embarrassed.

"Because you were asleep," I reply as she rolls her eyes at my excuse and gets up to get a donut. Of course the smell of donuts woke her, they've always been her favorite breakfast.

Dylan sits on the other side of Willow so I sit on my bed with Harley and Asher. Mav stays standing.

"Where's your roommate?" Mav asks while taking a bite of his donut getting chocolate icing all over the corners of his mouth.

"I'm not sure. I hope she's with her friends in one of their dorms because she never made her way back here last night," I say.

We eat in silence for the next couple of minutes all seemingly still distracted over the events of yesterday. "What do you think will happen now?" Dylan asks no one in particular. That question seems to be running through all of our heads. We don't know what to do because this has never happened before. Least of all at the university with all the guards patrolling.

"I don't have an answer to that one," Mav says.

"I hope they let us go home. At this point I just want to see my family," Willow replies.

"It'll be alright, you'll get to see them soon," Dylan comforts her, patting her shoulder. Jupiter is watching them and I feel like I catch a flicker of jealousy on his face, but it goes away as quickly as it came.

# Chapter 11

For the next two days, we don't have any classes. The guys decide to go back to Asher and Mav's dorm and stay there. Harley and Willow stay with me, but once again, Luna never comes back. I try her cell again, but still no answer, leaving me feeling very uneasy. As the day progresses, I decide to check the news site and find the names of everyone who died in the attack. Some of the people on the news are labeled as missing. My mind stops and my heart starts to race when I see Luna's name. I can't stop the tears from falling down my face. My hands start to shake and I can't see my phone in front of me anymore. I can't even process how Luna didn't make it. When was the last time I saw her? I can't think clearly to recall when that was. She is such a sweet person, she doesn't deserve any of this. No one did.

Three days after the attack, we are told that classes are starting back up again. All of us are feeling hesitant to go, which is understandable. Why the hell would I want to go back when the last time we were told it was safe, we got attacked by those things, so our lack of trust is not unfounded.

In the end we decide to go to class so we don't get in trouble. If we are told to go back it has to be safe, right? I'm just hoping everything will be alright. Harley and I walk Willow to her class before heading to ours, wanting to make sure she arrives safely. There's a heavy fog outside today causing me not to be able to see the other side of the courtyard and leaving us with an ominous feeling. We tell Willow before we leave that we'll meet her after class to walk back together, so she doesn't have to walk alone. Willow and Harley have basically become my new roommates.

With Luna gone and our uneasiness with the attack, we thought it would be a good idea to just stay together. The thought of Luna brings a pain in my heart. It hurts to know that I won't see her walk through the door again or how we won't get to play another game of cards together. I miss her so much and I didn't even know her for very long but I feel like we could have been great friends if we got that time together. But now she's gone and I won't get that chance.

We went to the girls' dorms one of the days we didn't have class to get some of their stuff to bring back to mine. I put all of Luna's things in a neat pile so I can give them to her family once they are allowed to come to campus and retrieve them.

If we will ever be able to leave.

Harley and I meet up with the guys before walking into the classroom. Jules is already sitting in her seat, but she looks different, not like her usual confident self. Instead, she is staring at her desk, her face showing no emotion like her mind is elsewhere. I walk up to my desk behind her and sit down.

"Jules?"

At the sound of her name, she perks up a little, but still doesn't turn around to face me.

"Jules?" I ask again.

Knowing who said her name now, she shifts in her seat so she is almost facing me. "Are you okay?" I ask.

She laughs sarcastically. "No actually, I'm not," she responds as she fully turns her body towards me. Her eyes are filled with tears. I am frozen, not knowing what to say or do. Even though I haven't known her for long, I never expected to see her crying. "My friends are dead. All of them! Not one of them made it. Those stupid things killed them all!" She sobs, losing all control she was trying to hold. "And now they're making us come back to these stupid classes after what happened?! What the hell? How are we supposed to pretend like nothing just happened?!"

She puts her elbows on her knees and her head in her hands where she loses all control. I gently rest my hand on her arm gently stroking her, trying to give some kind of comfort. I don't know if she is the type of person who likes physical touch so I don't know if she would want a hug right now, but I can't take it and wrap my arms around her shoulders. I hold her as her whole body shakes with sobs that hurt my heart just hearing them

"I'm so sorry to hear that, Jules. This is really tough right now, but just so you know, I see you and hear you and you shouldn't go through this alone. Why don't you stay with Harley, Willow and I?" I suggest.

Jules stays still for a moment, then she subtly nods her head. I slowly rub my thumb back and forth on her arm, as a way of continuing to comfort her and trying to show her she is not alone. She isn't pulling away from me so I guess she doesn't mind my comfort.

"I'm really sorry Jules. Even though we just met, we will help you get through this together. If there is anything you need just let us know and we will see what we can do," Harley tells her.

The others apologize and give Jules words of comfort. I take my hand off her arm and she turns back around in her seat.

Mr. Jacka walks into the classroom and heads towards his desk. I'm glad to know he's safe and alive. I can tell by looking around the classroom that there are less people than usual, so I try not to think too much about what that may mean. Since there are more seats open, Asher has moved closer to us.

Mr. Jacka writes our plans on the board then turns around and faces everyone. Some people around the room gasp as Mr. Jacka looks at us. I realize with a shock that his eyes are black, just like Mrs. Mason's eyes. He has no emotion showing on his face, which sends chills down my body and I start to feel my heart rate increasing as an uneasiness spreads through my body.

"Good morning class, it is good to see you all here. I know recent events have been tragic and sad, but it is good you still get your education in," Mr. Jacka says, but his voice is different. He is talking slower than usual, more monotone and flat sounding.

I look over at Harley and Jupiter, but they are already looking at me. Something is wrong here, I just can't figure out what. I'm not sure what the black eyes mean but they can't be good and they're creeping me out.

A girl with pretty chestnut skin and straight rich black hair raises her hand. "Yes?" Mr. Jacka says.

"Are you okay?" she boldly asks him.

Mr. Jacka just stares at her, his black eyes intensely looking at her. "I am perfectly fine. Just a little sick is all," his eyes never leave hers as he answers with a piercing stare. I get shivers just watching the exchange.

"O-okay. I just wanted to make sure," she quickly looks away from Mr. Jacka. After a few seconds, Mr. Jacka starts sharing our lesson plans.

After class, Mr. Jacka asks one of the students, Atticus, to stay after class. He gives a nervous glance around the room, then nods his head in answer. I don't have a good feeling about this. As I go to leave the room, I look back over my shoulder at Atticus. His bright blue eyes catch mine with a panicky look as everyone files out of the room. I find myself wanting to walk back to him so he isn't alone. However, one look at how Mr. Jacka stares at Atticus and that feeling leaves my body, replacing it with the fear of Mr. Jacka.

"What was that all about?" Asher asks me in a whisper as he walks beside me.

"I just have a weird feeling. I think I'm just being paranoid after everything that's happened," I reply, utterly confused and uneasy.

"Trust that feeling in your gut," Asher replies, leaving me feeling worse than before.

TWO NIGHTS LATER, WE all gather again to eat dinner together at the Zodiac grill, even Jules and Willow. I know it's risky to eat out, but I have to admit it's nice to go to a restaurant and not stay in the dorm room. Besides, there's a risk everywhere we go anyways. We've all gotten used to eating together every day so now it feels weird if we don't. Jules has been quiet and not herself recently, but I can't blame her. We've been giving her some space to try and process her grief, but also letting her know we are here for her to talk to us whenever she's ready.

Despite making it two full days without being attacked, somehow reports have been published stating that more people have died, including Atticus. No one saw him again after class that day and he didn't appear to be sick, so he had to have been murdered. The thought of Mr. Jacka crosses my mind but I quickly banish it, feeling guilty for not trusting my gut in the moment. Why is the staff only talking out the big attacks when there are smaller ones happening? Are they hoping to cause less speculation by not acknowledging it? All these questions flood my mind and I feel more uneasy about walking outside, but it's always better when I have someone with me. If I'm really honest and had a choice, I would stay in my dorm instead of going to class. Unfortunately, despite the continued deaths on campus, we are supposed to go to class and "continue our education" per the school administration.

After dinner, we all head back to Asher and Mav's dorm room. Some of us have to sit on the floor, but those sitting on beds offer pillows to sit on to those on the floor.

We are playing a card game when a scream comes from out in the hall. Everyone goes still, I don't even know if some of us are breathing. We all look at each other, unsure of what to do. Last time this happened, Asher and I had to climb out of a window while the dorm was attacked.

"We might want to go see if someone is in trouble," Asher whispers.

"Are you crazy? Last time we did that, we almost got killed. Maybe you bumped your head going through the window and forgot," I snap.

"Someone could be hurt or in danger right now. If we don't go find them, then we should go get the guards at least," he pleads back.

"I'll go with you. Better two of us than just one," Mav says. As he gets up from where he was sitting, he picks up a bat that is leaning in the corner of their room. "The rest of you should stay here. If worse comes to worse, find a way to get out through the windows."

"I'm going with you," I announce.

"No," Asher barks. "It's too dangerous."

"Oh, so it's too dangerous for me, but not for you two?" I growl back, my patience nonexistent. I stand there glaring with my arms crossed, waiting for him to answer. I don't know why I volunteered to go, but if they are helping, I want to go too. "Well, I'm going with you guys. End of discussion." I walk up to Mav and take the bat from his hands. Without thinking, I head out the door. I just hope I don't end up dead by the end of this.

The three of us head quietly down the hall when we hear another scream, more muffled this time, and follow the sound. The weird thing is, it sounds like only one person is screaming, so whatever these things are, if they are back, they must not be attacking everyone, which doesn't make sense. No one else is opening their doors or peeking their heads out, which is probably the smart thing to do. I'm starting to regret coming out here, but calm myself with thoughts that someone may need our help right now. Besides, if we run into one of those things, Mav or Asher can blast it with fire.

Mav walks in front of me, I'm in the middle, and Asher is in the back, the boys sandwiching me for safety. We come up to a corner and Mav carefully looks around it. He quickly jumps back and puts his back flush up against the wall, appearing to be frozen in fear.

"What did you see?" I whisper. Mav just nods his head in no. I quietly walk past him and peek around the corner myself while I feel someone grab at my waist trying to stop me.

The lights in the hall are on this time so I have a clear view of what is happening in front of me. A tall black figure stands above what appears to be a dead boy. Not just dead but...drained? The boy's face is pale, his lips are purple. His skin is so thin you can almost see his bones.

As if this couldn't get any scarier, the black figure appears to absorb into the boy's body. It just turned to this black fog and went into the boy's open mouth. The boy sounded like he sucked in a sharp breath and suddenly sat up. WHAT THE HELL? He slowly starts to look around and when he looks in my direction, I can see his eyes are black, just like Mrs. Mason and Mr. Jacka's are.

Just like Mav a few moments earlier I jump backwards with my back against the wall and whisper, "We need to go back, NOW!". Before they can answer, I take off sprinting down the hall.

As we run down the hall, I only hear the sound of my own gasping breathing and Mav and Asher's footsteps, but no one else's. Despite this I still don't feel relief because that thing could still be chasing us, not making any sounds when it moves. Then I realize the last time Asher and I got chased by one I *did* hear footsteps which gives me a fraction of relief.

We run quickly into the dorm room and slam the door in our rush to get inside, locking the door and collapsing to the floor. Harley jolts up from where she is sitting on the bed.

"What happened? Are any of you hurt?" she asks with anxiety in her voice.

Out of breath, Asher tries to say, "I don't know...what happened, I...didn't get to look. Blue...just told us...to get back here...so I did. Blue, what did you see?" He asks as he turns to look at me while still gasping for air.

I am leaning against the door, my body shaking, expecting to hear something banging on it any second from the other side. When that doesn't happen, I take a calming breath and try to answer. I explained to them every detail of what I saw in the hallway including how the boy's eyes turned black. Mav tells them he saw something similar to the beginning of what I saw regarding the black figure standing over what appeared to be a dead boy, but he didn't see anything after that.

"So you're saying, one of those creatures now lives in that boy's body?" Jules asks us. Her face has a scared and shocked expression on it as her color drains to a ghostly white shade. Her hands are clenched in fist and her whole body is tense.

"Basically, yes," I reply. We all stare at each other in silence. I realize I'm holding my breath still expecting to hear banging on the door. This reminds me too much of the time Asher and I were attacked. I hate this. I go to say as much to the group when my thoughts are interrupted.

"What if we go to the library?" Jupiter suggests. "Maybe we could look up some things, you know, do some research while we are there and see if we find anything that can tell us about what is happening."

"I mean, maybe. What would we even look for though? I'm pretty sure this has never happened before...like in the history of the world," Harley says.

"I think it's worth a shot. What's the worst that could happen? We go to a library and find nothing," Dylan tells everyone.

"Actually, the worst that could happen would be that we get killed on the way there probably," Mav says. Everyone just looks at him shocked that he is voicing out loud what we were all probably already thinking, but afraid to admit. "What? I'm just saying," he replies.

"Dude, really?" Harley rolls her eyes and looks back at everyone else.

"I think we should go. If we don't find anything, then we come back," Asher says.

"I don't know if I want to go out in the hall with that thing roaming around," Willow says. When I look over at her, I can tell she is uncomfortable. She is fidgeting with her fingers and bouncing her leg.

"We are on the side of the building that has a fire escape just outside the window," Mav reminds everyone. I can't help but think to myself that's good because I don't want to climb down the bed sheets again if we need to escape in a rush when I realize Mav is actually suggesting we all leave that way to go to the library. He heads towards the window to climb out and we all follow him.

Everyone climbs down the fire escape, but no one says a word. Once everyone is down, we quietly start walking towards the library. The library probably isn't open now so if we are going to do this, we may have to find a way to get in.

"You know, maybe we should go tomorrow. The chances of us getting killed by one of those things during the night is probably higher than during the day don't you think? When I said we should go to the library, I didn't really mean tonight," Jupiter whispers to everyone with a nervous edge to his voice.

"Well, if you didn't mean tonight you should have said something before we left," Asher bites back with annoyance.

"Well, I didn't know it would be this creepy. There is so much fog everywhere, more than usual, I can't see a damn thing," Jupiter states. He is right, the fog makes it hard to see what's in front of us.

"We are already outside so let's just keep moving," I announce.

We make it to the library and just like I feared, the doors are locked. "Step back everyone, I got this," Jules says. She sounded more like her confident self when she said that, making me look surprised in her direction.

Jules steps up to the door and holds up both her arms with her palms out pointing at the door handles. She uses her air power to blow a gust of wind into the lock, opening it somehow. Impressive. When she pushes the doors open, they make a loud creaky sound.

Lanterns started to turn on one by one, showing the rows and rows of bookshelves. I know that the main desk is located in the middle of the library since I came here once to look for books.

"Where are we supposed to start?" I ask as I realize we are all standing outside, just looking in.

"Well for starters, we should probably go inside," Harley says. I give an annoyed look towards her and she just smiles back.

"Maybe let's start with history or ancient history. Maybe an incident like this happened before and we never learned about it," Jupiter suggests.

"I think if something like this were to ever have happened, we would definitely know about it," Asher tells Jupiter.

We all walk inside and head towards the history section. As we walk, more lanterns start to automatically turn on. I realize they must be motion censored. In the middle of the history section of the library, there is a wooden table with stacks of books on it and chairs all around.

"We will just look around for a bit and see if we can find anything," I announce.

After at least twenty minutes of researching no one was finding a single piece of information about what or why this is happening or what those things even are.

While looking over a book, Jupiter says, "Did you guys know that Umbra means the fully shaded inner region of a shadow cast by an opaque object. So Umbra University is basically the Shadow University."

"It's kind of creepy that the name of the university basically means that and the things attacking us are like shadows. It could be related somehow," Harley says.

We keep researching and reading books for a bit longer when Mav suddenly sits up in his seat. "I may have found something!"

"What?" I ask as everyone gathers around the chairs near Mav.

"What did you find?" says a raspy voice. I look to where it came from, but I can't seem to find a source. Everyone starts to get up out of their chairs.

"Who's there?" Asher asks suddenly as we all realize we are not alone.

On the opposite end of the table, someone emerges from the bookshelves. No, not someone, it is one of the shadow creatures. To the right, another one comes out of the shadows. I notice that the shadow creatures actually have a mouth that is all black like a void. You can almost not see it since it blends in with its body. It only seems to have a mouth though, no eyes, nose or ears. Ugh, creepy.

More and more of the shadow creatures start to come out of the bookshelves. I really hope I am sleeping right now and this is just a nightmare, not happening in real life.

"I was hoping to have a midnight snack," the shadow creature that came out first says. It moves its head like it is looking over all of us then it abruptly stops at me. "How about you first?"

Before I could even react, this black fog looking stuff came shooting from the creature's body towards me.

"Blue!" someone yells.

I don't even have time to respond or react when I feel myself getting tackled to the floor moments before the fog can reach me. "Holy shit Blue, are you okay?" Asher asks quickly after pushing me out of the way of that magic stuff and we land huddled together on the floor.

"I'm fine. Thanks," I reply, short of breath and trying to figure out what the heck is happening.

A boy about our age appears. Initially I think he's like us, but his eyes give him away. In what feels like slow motion a shadow creature emerges from his body and the boy falls to the ground like an empty shell of a human.

"Run!" Mav yells.

Asher basically hauls me off the ground and we take off running, separating us from everyone else. One of the shadow creatures appears in front of us and Asher instinctively blasts it with his fire. It makes a loud shrieking noise upon impact and we take this opportunity to quickly rush past it. If only I was outside, then I could use my earth power to help us against this thing, I feel useless.

As we run, I can hear the bookshelves being run into by something and the loud thud as books fall to the ground. I realize those things must have been trying to be silent before so we wouldn't hear them approaching us, but since we know they're here, there's no need to hide or be quiet in their pursuit of us.

Running through the library is like running through a maze trying to find the way out. I don't even remember the direction we came from let alone where the nearest exit is. I can't seem to concentrate and I start to feel my panic rising. Someone starts screaming from a distance and I hear a gush of wind before I feel it. My stomach drops at the feel and I think to myself that this can't be good.

In my panic I trip over a stack of books. Asher instantly grabs my arm and helps steady me. "Keep moving," he tells me in a calm voice. I honestly have no clue how he can be so calm right now. I feel like I'm about to have a panic attack. My heart is racing and feels like it will beat out of my chest while I struggle to get air in my lungs.

As we run, Asher keeps a hand on my arm, making sure I stay with him. He pulls me down what we expect to be another aisle of books, but it's not an aisle, but a freaking dead end. There are no lanterns on so it's pitch black back here.

"What are you..." but before I can finish my sentence, he pulls me down to the floor with him. Asher's back is against one of the bookshelves and I'm sitting with my back to him, up against his chest in-between his legs.

I may have been focused on those shadow creatures before, but now all I focus on is how close Asher and I are. I can't help but feel every place his body touches mine. He has both his arms wrapped around my waist. I can feel his breath on my neck, causing all the hair on my body to stand on end, momentarily distracting me from what's going on.

We stay silent as we hear footsteps coming our way. I snap out of my Asher daze and realize those things have to have feet if they can make footsteps or maybe it's in a human body now, or worse. Not just any human body, but what if it's one of the others I think in a panic.

"Come out, come out wherever you are," it says. I can hear it coming closer and closer. It feels like I'm in a horror movie right now and I absolutely hate the sheer panic coursing through my body. I may enjoy watching these movies, but I never ever wanted to actually live in one.

"I wish I had that bat right about now," I whisper. Asher's' quiet chuckle vibrates through my body.

Having Asher hold me like this has given me a safe feeling that I haven't felt in a while. I won't even lie, it feels nice to feel protected even if we aren't really in a situation to feel that way.

"Do you hear that?" Asher whispers in my ear as he leans forward and presses more firmly against my back.

I listen for a second. "What? I hear nothing," I whisper back.

"Exactly," Right at that moment, the shadow creature that had been following us jumps out in front of the bookshelf, charging towards us.

Asher holds his arms up in front of me and blasts fire from his hands. We both quickly stand up and start running. As we run past the shadow creature that is burning, it crashes into a bookshelf in its attempt to rid the fire from its body. It quickly pushes itself away from the shelf before anything catches on fire.

"I don't know how this place has not caught on fire from your blast," I say as we run.

"Do you really doubt my abilities?" Asher asks.

"Maybe," I answered. Before he can reply, I take off faster.

I start to feel like we are almost safe when something grabs my arm. It is cold against my warm skin. I'm yanked back, away from Asher and I bump against something hard and freezing cold giving me chills all the way to my bones. I look over my shoulder and find one of the shadow creatures has gotten a hold of me. I try to fight out of its grasp, but it digs its long claws in my arms. I scream from the intense pain. It feels like someone is digging into my skin with cold knives and my arm is being torn apart when my vision starts to turn black.

Suddenly the creature lets go of me and I feel myself fall to the floor. What is happening? Why did it let go? I feel my skin get hot for a second, then cold again. Something wet is dripping down my arm.

Someone's hands are on my shoulders and I tense away. My vision isn't completely back, only allowing me to see figures. "It's me, Blue. It's me," a silhouette takes form and Asher is leaning over me. He has a cut on his forehead and there's blood dripping down his face. I try to reach up to touch it, but my arm feels too heavy. "We have to keep going, we're almost there," he says with sincerity and concern in his eyes.

Asher helps me to my feet as best he can, but as we start to run again my whole body feels heavy and uneasy. The more we move the more my senses seem to slowly be coming back.

I feel a jolt of hope as I see the exit is just ahead, but my excitement quickly changes to panic, as I hear another creature gaining on us again. I know I'm slowing us down, but Asher stays by my side. I'm tempted to tell him to go ahead without me, but I know he's too stubborn to listen. The creature blasts its black fog in between Asher and I, making it hard to see each other.

We both bolt out the doors as fast as we can. I look behind me to find the shadow creature still chasing us. I harness what energy is left in me and use my power to make a big ball of dirt from the ground, throwing it at the creature, then without a moment's hesitation immediately make another one. Again and again as more creatures appear, I repeat making and throwing these dirt balls at the creature in quick succession all while Asher blasts them with his fire.

A gust of wind knocks the last of the creatures attacking us down from behind. Looking up at the doors I find Jules, Dylan and Mav running out, one last creature chasing them. Asher sees the creature following them and quickly attacks, burning it before it can reach them. We all watch as the creature shrieks and turns into ashes.

I look back at the others and notice they have some cuts on their faces and arms, but they don't seem to have any major injuries.

"Thank goodness you guys are alright. Where are the others?" I gasp with relief and exhaustion.

"We don't know. We got separated from you guys so we thought they were with you," Dylan answers with concern on his face.

As we hear heavy footsteps coming from inside the library everyone gets into a fighting stance, one Mr. Watson taught us in class. But instead of one of the shadow creatures running out, Harley, Jupiter and Willow are there instead and relief floods my body.

Once they are all out, Jupiter quickly turns around and shuts the doors. Creatures start to bang on the doors from inside the library while Jupiter tries to hold them shut.

"Could use a little help here," he gasps and we all rush to help Jupiter hold the door shut.

As we work together to hold the door closed, Asher says, "Open the door on three."

"What?" everyone asks in shocked unison. My arm is throbbing from earlier, but I ignore it as I try to make sense of what Asher is instructing us to do.

"Just do what he says," Mav pipes in and Asher nods his head at Mav, a look of understanding passing between them.

"1...2...3," everyone lets go and tumbles backwards.

Before the creatures could get one step outside the library, Mav and Asher blast them with their fire as we watch in awe as they destroy one after another turning to ash. Once they are all gone, we slowly get to our feet breathless and looking around at each other in shock.

"Blue, your arm," Harley's face is full of concern.

I look down to find my arm bleeding and a bit torn up and suddenly get the overwhelming feeling I'm going to faint. Someone catches me before I can hit the ground.

"Easy there. It's alright. You'll be fine," Asher reassures me in a soothing tone while he gently sets me on the ground and kneels next to me. Mav kneels on my other side and carefully takes a look at my arm.

"We need to get her to the healing center," Mav announces.

"Willow too," Jupiter says. We all look over at Willow to find her sitting on the ground with scratches on her legs and arms.

"What happened?" Dylan asks as he runs over to her then kneels beside her.

"One of those *things* got a hold of her," Jupiter explains.

"Enough talking. Let's get them to the healing center," Jules says while helping me up.

We try to get there as fast as we can, but with everyone's injuries it takes a bit longer than we hoped. When we walk in, a nurse comes running up to us, asking what happened.

"We got attacked by strange creatures," Asher explains. The nurse doesn't ask anymore questions, but takes us to a room big enough to fit everyone. We're probably not the first students to walk in here with these types of injuries.

While one of the nurses is working on cleaning and suturing my arm, I notice Mav has a book under his arm. I didn't see that he had it before, but he must have grabbed it when everyone started to run.

"What do you have there Mav?" I ask.

"I'll tell you later," he says, returning back to watching another nurse working on Willow and her injuries.

Jules turns around to look at him with an annoyed expression on her face. "Is that what you risked your life running back to get? That stupid book?" Jules is in a special mood right now.

Mav has a concerned look on his face as he processes Jules' anger. I will have to remind myself never to get on her bad side or I'll face the consequences.

"Number one, it's not *stupid*! Books are very important when it comes to gaining knowledge. Number two, this one is especially important because it has some of the information we are looking for," Mav yells. Taking a deep breath, seeming to calm himself down, he continues, "But like I said, I'll explain more once we get out of here."

Once my arm is done being wrapped and Willow is done being treated, we head back to my dorm. The nurses gave me some pain killers and said my arm is still going to ache, but it will heal over time. I will just have to continue to wrap my arm in the new clean gauze they gave me.

A couple of guards walk us back to my dorm building and I feel better with them around. When we get back, I lay down on my bed, exhausted from tonight's events. Everyone piles in the room, finding a comfortable spot, because there is no way in hell we are staying in our separate rooms. We are all still on edge and trying to process what just happened.

"Will you now explain why the book you have is so important?" Jules asks. Mav takes the book out and scrolls through the pages, stopping on the one he needs.

"Before we got interrupted, I found something that I think we will all find very useful. This book basically provides information about all the creatures that roamed through our lands before we were even born. I found something that is similar to the black shadow creatures that are haunting us now," Mav pauses and looks up to see everyone's eyes on him. "They're demons. It gives a description of what they look like and it even has a drawing. I swear it is the exact same thing we have been seeing on campus attacking us." He holds the book up for everyone to see and sure enough, they look exactly like the shadow creatures.

"Demons!" Harley yells. "We are being attacked by freaking demons!"

"Holy shit dude," Asher stands up and starts to pace back and forth in the room.

"The university is possessed by demons," Jules says in a strangely calm voice. "Perfect."

"Oh my god. Oh my god. Oh my god," Jupiter repeats this over and over again while pacing the room. Willow and I stay silent. I don't even know what to say as I process the fact we have literally been getting attacked by demons. I didn't even know demons were real, they've always seemed like a myth.

"What do we do? The demons have been killing everyone they can get their hands, or should I say, claws on. I almost got killed by a demon! More than once! I could have been possessed by one just like freaking Mrs. Mason! Mrs. Mason, oh my god she's possessed by a demon," Harley rambles.

"Shit. God, oh god you guys. This literally can't be happening. This just can't, oh my god," Jupiter says in a panic as he falls back onto the bed. I can see his hands shaking as he run them over his face. Dylan and Willow are next to him as Dylan quietly whispers to Willow. His hand rests on top of hers and when Jupiter sees this he quickly sits back up, looking at their hands then up at them. "It'll be okay Willow, we'll all be fine," Dylan says.

"What are we supposed to do?" I ask the group. My voice came out surprisingly calm even though I'm freaking out on the inside, feeling the furthest thing from calm.

"We shouldn't attend class anymore. Any one of our professors could be possessed and we just can't risk it," Dylan declares.

"We need to research more. Find out more information about the demons," Jules tells Mav.

"I'll keep looking through the book. It probably has some more useful info in here that we probably need to know," Mav starts methodically looking for more information slowly flipping through the pages. Until we learn more, no one knows what to do next. Demons are literally walking around campus. When I talked about coming here, this was the last thing I expected to happen.

"We should probably get some sleep," Asher suggests.

"If I'm being honest, I don't really want to go back out there. I'm not in the mood for another attack," Jupiter says.

"Maybe we could make do here? Two people per bed and two people can sleep in between the beds on the floor then there is enough room by the bottom of the beds, near the door, for the rest of us to sleep. It'll be a tight squeeze but we'll make do. We have extra blankets and all that," I suggest.

"That could work," Asher says. "How about two guys sleep in one bed and two girls in the other? The rest are on the ground with blankets."

"I'll be fine on the floor," Jules tells everyone as she grabs a blanket and starts to make a spot for herself between the beds.

"How about Harley and Willow in my bed? Mav and Dylan in the other. Is that okay with everyone?" I ask.

"That works," Jupiter says.

Mav puts the book down and gets into bed, Dylan next to him. Jupiter starts to make a spot for himself next to Jules in-between the beds leaving Asher and I to sleep near the bottom of the beds. We lay horizontally, Asher closest to the door.

I don't know how long it takes me to fall asleep, but it feels like I lay here for hours. I didn't even know I was asleep until I startle awake from a nightmare as images of demons flash through my mind. I hear someone sniffle, like they're crying, so I slowly sit up and peek over the bed to find Willow sitting on the edge of the bed with her head in her hands.

Jupiter is sitting next to her with an arm around her. Willow moves her head to rest it on Jupiter's shoulder, seeking comfort. I feel like this is probably something I shouldn't intrude on so I quietly lay back down. Soon after, I fell back asleep.

# Chapter 12

I'm running through the library again. How did I get here? The demons are chasing me and they're closer this time. I look over to find Asher running next to me while blood is running down the side of his head.

"Asher, your head," I pant as we keep running.

"I'm fine. Keep moving," he demands.

We continue to run for what feels like hours. My legs are burning and my lungs can't seem to get enough air. We keep turning left, right, left, right, but the exit never appears. I desperately want to stop to catch my breath but I don't want the demons to take me.

"You can't escape from us," says a raspy voice. A demon's voice. "You will never be able to leave. You will never be able to see your family again, especially your dear sister."

What the hell?! How does it know I have a sister? It's becoming even harder to breathe. "No, you're wrong! We will make it, we will get out!" At that moment, when we take another right, the exit appears in front of us.

"See, we're going to make it!" I say. I didn't realize that was a lie.

I look to my right to find one of the demons grab Asher and pull him behind. I turn around and watch as the demon digs its claws in him. His scream of agony brings me to my knees.

"ASHER!!!" I scream as darkness swarms around me causing the exit to disappear, panicking when I lose sight of him. I can't hear him anymore. What if he's dead?

"You will never get away," the demon says again.

We didn't make it.

I jerk awake, trying to bring air in my lungs. I must have been holding my breath. I look over at the window where I see the sun is starting to come up. I bring my knees up to my chest and wrap my arms around them, resting my head on my knees. I finally gain control of my breathing and my heart beat is slowing down.

It was just a nightmare, it wasn't real. Out of nowhere, a hand is placed on my shoulder. I jerk out of the hand's reach and look over to find Asher sitting up, looking at me with concern.

"It's okay, just me. Sorry, I didn't mean to scare you like that. Are you okay?" he whispers. I breathed a sigh of relief knowing now that it was just him and not a demon. I'm still a bit shook so all I can do is nod my head yes. I rest my back against the base of the bed as Asher moves and sits next to me.

"Do you want to talk about it?" he asks.

"No," I reply. We sit in silence for a while, but not the awkward type, it actually feels nice sitting next to him. I close my eyes and imagine my parents and Emily back at home. I remember memories of my family and Harley going boating on the lake. Harley and I would always love to go tubing. My dad would always try to knock us off by doing really sharp turns on the boat and he would always succeed, every time. Thinking of him makes my heart miss him. I just need one of those big bear hugs from him right now.

"What are we going to do?" Asher asks, interrupting my thoughts.

"I don't know," I answer. "I was never expecting this to happen. I just hope everything outside the university is okay."

"Me too. There would probably be information on the news about it if there was trouble outside," Asher says.

"I mean, what is even happening? This is just all crazy shit. What if this is just a nightmare? What if it's still the day before I came here?" I ask, already knowing the answer.

"It's not a dream Blue. It's our reality, but we'll make it through this, together," He takes my hand in his and squeezes it as disappointment crashes through me.

"But what if we don't make it through this?" I ask. I take my hand out of his grasp and put both my hands over my face. I try to hold my tears from falling but it doesn't work. My breathing turns erratic at the thought of never seeing my family again.

"Blue, look at me," Asher orders. I don't listen and I keep my hands on my face, not wanting him to see me like this. "Blue." After waiting a few seconds and realizing I won't look at him, he takes my wrists and moves them away from my face. When I look at him, his face is inches from mine.

"We are going to get through this, all of us. Every single person in this room is strong and none of us will give up, so you shouldn't either," he tells me. "Okay?" I nod my head yes. He doesn't move away, his hands move to hold my face.

My face starts to become warm and I'm pretty sure I'm blushing. Asher is looking deeply into my eyes. "Have I ever told you how beautiful you are?" he whispers.

I stay silent for a moment, processing what he has said. "No," I whisper back.

"Well you are, so very beautiful. Both inside and out," his eyes look down at my lips then back at my eyes, as if asking for permission.

I nod my head and before I know it, his lips are on mine. It feels like time stops when he kisses me. The butterflies in my stomach seem to be going crazy. My heart skips a beat. The only thing I can focus on is how soft his lips are. I move my hand behind his head, my fingers getting tangled in his hair. It feels as though Asher and I are the only two people in this world, let alone this room.

We both pull back, catching our breaths. I have kissed a boy before, but it never felt as passionate as this does with Asher.

"You weren't that bad," Asher jokes with a sexy grin on his adorable face.

"Oh whatever," I say laughing. I give him a playful shove in the shoulder.

"I'm just kidding," he says as he grabs the arm I shove him with. My arm tingles from where he touches me. "I love it when you smile. It lights up this beautiful face of yours," he leans in and rests his forehead against mine. "I've wanted to do that for quite some time now." We both close our eyes and sit there, in a comfortable silence. It's crazy how comfortable I feel around Asher, even if we didn't get along at first, there is definitely a part of me that feels safe with him.

"We should probably get more sleep. Never know what tomorrow holds," Asher says.

"I don't know if I'll be able to sleep," I confess. From the nightmare to the kiss my body is completely awake now. It will definitely take me a while to fall back asleep.

Asher sits back against the bed. "Well then just rest your head on my shoulder and close your eyes," I do as he says, moving closer to him. When I am settled in, Asher rests his head on mine and starts rubbing my back.

I can't believe I just kissed Asher. Asher King just kissed me! What the heck is going on? I recognize now that my feelings for Asher go beyond friendship and if I'm really honest, probably have from the beginning, but I never wanted to acknowledge it. Now that I have, I know I've actually started to like Asher, started to see him as more than an annoying classmate. I just never realized it until now. When I was sitting in-between his legs in the library, he actually made me feel safe. We may have gotten off on the wrong foot, but that's exactly how I feel around him, like I can be my true self and he won't back away.

It was easier to fall asleep that night snuggled up with Asher. At one point, Asher pulls me closer to him. It's a good thing he was asleep so he couldn't see me blushing.

WHEN I WAKE UP THE next morning, I find Jules already awake. Seeing Asher's arm wrapped tightly around me she gives a cocky grin and mouths *I knew it*. I just roll my eyes and smile. It's good to see her smile again.

Once everyone is up, Mav says, "We need to get more books from the library to research."

"No way in hell I'm going back there," Jupiter says.

"It's daytime and other people may be in there. I doubt the demons will attack us during the day," Mav keeps pushing.

"Really, you don't, because I distinctly remember one time during class when it was light outside and we got attacked, or do you not remember?"

"Someone is in a mood today," Harley mumbles.

Jupiter takes a deep breath. "Sorry, I'm just tired and hungry. I get angry on an empty stomach."

"So you're hangry?" Jules asks while giving him a big grin.

"Let's not push his buttons. We can go get food and then decide if we want to go to the library again," I tell everyone.

After we find some food and eat, we decide that whoever doesn't want to go to the library can stay back in the dorm.

"I think I will stay. I don't want to go back there for a while," Willow says. She is sitting on the edge of the bed, fidgeting with her hands. It dawns on me just then that I don't know much about Willow. I haven't really had the time to sit down and talk with her. I take a note to privately talk with her in the future, if we have one.

"I'll stay back with Willow so she's not alone. The rest of you can go on," Dylan announces.

"Alright, then it's settled," says Jules. Everyone other than Willow and Dylan start to get ready. I look over at Jupiter and catch what appears to be a jealous look on his face. He is staring at Willow and Dylan, watching them talk about something. Obviously, there is something going on between them however it's really none of my business.

Harley, Jules and I head to the community bathroom to get ready. There are very few people here now. I don't know if that's from so many people staying in their dorms or just...from the lack of students here in light of recent events.

Once everyone is ready to go, we head out into a light fog surrounding the campus and I assume it probably has something to do with the demons. Now when I think back, the fog started to appear when the murders started to happen.

We all stand in front of the library doors, hesitant to go in. The few students that are outside give us strange looks and I have no doubt that we look really suspicious right now. They may think we are possessed because we are just standing here.

"Um Asher? Did you really bring a bat to the library? What's that going to do? They can literally shred that thing with their claws." Harley asks. On the way here, we stopped at the Aries dorms and Asher ran in the building and came out with the bat.

"Self-defense," he replies. We haven't talked about last night, but I hope we can maybe clarify what is happening between us. I know we aren't *just friends* anymore but what are we?

"You can freaking throw fire out of your hands. You are the last person who needs that bat right now. Blue and I can't even use our powers in there."

"If this is your way of asking for the bat then you're doing a pretty bad job of it," Asher holds the bat out for Harley to grab.

"Harley takes it from his hand. "Shut up."

"Can we just go in already, I want to get this over with," Jules says with her arms crossed. She looks around the greens, as if expecting a demon to appear any minute.

"Same. I want to get back to the dorm as soon as possible," Jupiter says. I have a feeling his reasoning has more to do with the people back at the dorm than fear of the demons showing up.

"Alrighty grumpy pants, let's go," Mav says to them while walking inside. Everyone else follows close behind. Hopefully this experience will be better since we won't have lanterns as our only light source.

"As soon as I see anything suspicious, I'm out of here," Harley announces.

"I'll be right behind you," says Jupiter.

I notice that Asher is never far away from me, which makes me feel better knowing he is close by. This time, when we look through the books, we know what to look more closely for. I discover a children's book with a demon as the villain, though I'm not sure it will be helpful. I see someone walk out from the bookshelves and I immediately stand up.

"Settle down everyone. It's just me," the librarian walks by us and back into the bookshelves. She looks to be just passing by and when she gets close, I notice her eyes aren't black which is good because it means despite the demons having been here yesterday, they didn't attack her. I wonder if she knows if they were here?

We all wait in tense silence for anything unusual to happen. When nothing does, everyone relaxes and we all go back to looking through the books.

"In this book of myths, it talks about how demons have been lurking in our world for centuries, they have just been in hiding, until now I guess. It says that there is a demon leader named Morthil. Morthil controls everything the demons do," Harley explains.

"I wouldn't be surprised if that's all true because they're clearly here on campus," Jupiter asks. "Do you think Morthil could possibly be here?"

"It might be, but Morthil could be a myth. We just can't tell if it's real or some made up theory," says Asher. "Yet, after all we have been through, I wouldn't be surprised if he showed up at our doorstep one day."

"In my book it talks about how much demons hate fire, which I think we already know. It says they prefer darkness over daylight. So I assume they will probably attack more at night," Jules shares with everyone.

We spend about an hour at the library, trying to locate things that can help us, but all we find is the description of what they look like, they hate fire and prefer the dark, and that Morthil is their leader.

As we leave the library, we checkout some books to take with us. We decide to warn the librarian that demons were here last night. She just waves off our warning and tells us that if they haven't come for her yet, they probably don't plan on it.

During the walk back to the dorm, we discuss more about our findings. We try not to be too loud in case someone or something is listening because you never know what lurks in the shadows. In one of the books I was reading, it explains some of the things the demons have done in the past, how they have haunted humans. Reading more about what they've done makes my fear of them grow. How will we ever survive this?

When we get to the Aries dorm, Mav says something about grabbing blankets and pillows since we should just stay in my dorm room from now on instead of being separated. We hurry inside their dorm and grab all the things we will need. When we get back to my dorm room, Willow and Dylan are still sitting on the bed. We drop the blankets and pillows in a corner of the room, on the ground.

"Willow and I were thinking that maybe we can go to the training facility to get some weapons. Mr. Watson at least taught us self-defense and that will definitely come in handy," Dylan tells everyone.

"We don't need weapons, we have our powers," Jules says.

"We can't always rely on our powers to save us. Who knows if demons possess the ability to take them away. I wouldn't be surprised,"

Asher says to Jules. "We can go to the training facility and ask for Mr. Watson's permission before taking the weapons."

"I don't think he has a class now so we won't be bothering him," Mav shares. "Even if he did, people probably aren't even showing up to it."

WHEN WE ARRIVE AT THE training facility, none of the lights are on. It's so dark we can't see inside the building. I don't want to walk in there with the lights off after finding out demons prefer the dark, they could be hiding in there right now.

"Isn't Mr. Watson supposed to be here?" Harley asks.

"He could be in his quarters in the back," Mav suggests. Mr. Watson doesn't stay at the professors building, but has his own quarters here at the training facility.

"Mr. Watson?" Asher yells.

"What the hell do you think you're doing? Trying to bring the demons to us?" Jupiter asks.

"If there are really demons in here, they would have seen or heard us by now," Asher explains. Asher cups his mouth with his hands and yells, "Mr. Watson!" His voice echoes off the walls but there is no reply.

"He probably can't hear us from the back. We can just turn the lights on," Dylan says. Dylan walks up to the entrance but pauses, takes a deep breath, and hesitantly walks in.

"Dylan wait," Willow tries to reach for him but he is already out of view. A few moments later, the lights all turn on one by one. Everyone walks in and calls for Mr. Watson.

"Hello everyone," I turn around and see Mr. Watson standing behind us.

"Jeez Mr. Watson, you almost made me shit my pants," Jupiter chuckles but then stops suddenly. He stares at Mr. Watson with wide eyes. I turn my head to see what he is looking at. Nothing seems off about him except for...his eyes that are black. Shit.

"Mr. Watson, what happened to you?" Willow whispers.

"Look at you," Mr. Watson takes a step towards Willow. "All nice and *delicious*," he gets closer and closer to Willow.

Jupiter steps in front of her, blocking Mr. Watson's way. "You are not going to lay a single finger on her, you understand?" The joking, funny Jupiter we all love just disappeared. Instead, he has the most serious look I've ever seen on his face. Mr. Watson just gives Jupiter a devil's smile.

The demon inside his body emerges outside of his body and Mr. Watson falls to the floor. I can't tell if he is alive, unconscious or dead, but I know he's not moving.

"Really?" The demon asks. "And what are you, a weak little human boy, going to do to stop me?" The demon stops where it is and folds its black arms across its chest. Black mist floats around its body. We've never been around a demon this long without it attacking us.

"I-" Jupiter looks around the room. He picks up a knife from the shelf. "I'll kill you."

The demon tosses its head back and makes an ugly laughing sound. "With that thing?" The demon stops laughing suddenly. "I'd like to see you try," and without a warning, the demon pounces at Jupiter.

Everything happens so fast. Willow jumps out of the way while the demon tackles Jupiter. The knife falls out of his hand and tumbles across the floor. Dylan is quick to grab another knife off the rack. Harley reaches out and Dylan hands it to her.

The demon and Jupiter wrestle on the ground. Jupiter is trying to keep the demon's claws away from him so it doesn't scratch him.

"Jupiter!" Harley yells. She slides the knife across the floor towards him and with lightning speed Jupiter grabs it and stabs the demon. As the demon stumbles off him, it gives Jupiter enough time to wiggle out of its grip freeing himself.

I look away from the fight to find more demons suddenly appearing out from the shadows around the room. "Where the hell did they come from?" I say. Everyone is quick to grab a weapon.

The demons start to attack us from all sides. I do my best to fight them off, but I'm not as experienced in combat as I should be for this situation. You can tell Asher, Dylan and Mav are more skilled than the rest of us just by the way they fight and move with the knives and swords. It must be from growing up in Gena and living in the woods. I faintly remember them mentioning how they've trained together before.

Jupiter sticks by Willow's side and helps her fend the demons away. Willow does her best to use the dagger she has in her hand but you can tell she is inexperienced, like me, and she hesitates when using the dagger.

Every time I get rid of one demon, another one comes at me. I don't get a break as they keep appearing. I quickly learn that stabbing them doesn't seem to kill them, just wounds them. Asher and Mav are using their firepower to kill the demons, which seems to be the only way to make that happen.

"You stupid fire-benders," I hear a demon say.

Out of the corner of my eye, I watch as one of the demons' dark magic shoots across the room. It wraps around Mav's body, making it so he can't move.

"I'm sick and tired of this shit," Mav says while writhing within the shadows. Fire explodes around his body causing the demon's grip to loosen. "I was hoping just a sword and dagger can defeat you guys but I guess not," he says. Mav goes all out, blasting most of the demons with fire and their screams pierce the air. How have none of the University guards heard any of this? I feel like I haven't seen a guard in weeks so have the demons killed them or are they possessed?

Being inside the building, I can't use my power unless I'm close to the exit, but I feel completely useless just using a dagger. I suddenly realize there is something I could try to do that may help, but it will take lots of focus and energy. I edge towards the exit hoping I just have to get a little closer for this to work. Once I'm in range, I make boulders of dirt float in the air. Then, using most of my energy, I turn the boulders into human forms. It takes all of my concentration and a headache already starts to form. I imagine the way I want them to look. Once they are formed, I make the dirt creatures walk into the building. One of the demons notices them and comes charging towards one. I command the dirt creature, making it punch the demon in the gut, sending it flying back. A smile starts to spread across my face as I realize this may actually work.

Soon there are more demons attacking me and the dirt creatures causing me to start losing control, making the dirt creatures weaker, ultimately allowing the demons to break them down, one by one. I'm so focused on making more dirt creatures, I don't notice a demon throwing one of them right at me sending me flying backwards. My back hits a wall and sharp pain shoots its way up my spine. As I struggle to my feet, I see the same demon send its dark magic racing towards me. I try my best to get up as fast as I can to avoid being hit, but before it can reach me, the magic gets blasted with a fireball. I look to my right to find Asher running towards me. He helps me to my feet and we fight side by side, our backs up against each other. I'm starting to feel exhausted but tell myself I can't give up yet. I have to ignore the pain for now if i want to stay alive.

I don't know how long we have been fighting for, but I realize none of the university guards have shown up. I would have run to try and find one but I can't leave the others here and the reality is who the heck knows if I would even find one of them. As I look across the fight you can tell everyone is starting to get tired because our technique is becoming sloppy.

Just then Jupiter gets tossed across the room, away from Willow. The demon's magic wraps around her, holding her so tight that she can't move and simultaneously lifts her off the ground as she struggles against the grip. I follow the magic to see which demon is controlling it. Once I find the right one, I run towards it but another demon steps in my path, blocking my way. The demon hits me with its arm, sending me across the room. I land hard on my back, again, the pain is even worse as it radiates across my body. I think someone is yelling my name but I can't tell. I try to get back up but the pain is too much. Not knowing how badly injured my back is and not wanting to make it worse, I lay back down as carefully as I can, hoping no demon will come and kill me.

I turn my head to the side and watch as Willow gets carried towards the exit. Jupiter is struggling to get up, just like I was. He crawls towards her but he is too slow. Everyone else is busy fighting other demons that no one can help Willow as she is carried away. Dylan is the only other person to see Willow being stolen away so tries to get to her too, but he is surrounded and doesn't make any progress.

The demon's magic carries Willow out the exit, away from view. "Willow! Willow no!" Jupiter yells. He tries to get up again but falls back down.

"This can't be happening," I say. I try to get up again but I can only sit on my knees now. I lean over resting my hands on the floor, taking deep breaths as the pain starts to fade. Nothing seems to be broken, I just feel sore everywhere and cannot control my movements to get my body in motion.

The demons start to retreat towards the exit. Mav, Asher and Dylan follow them and blast them with fire, but out of nowhere, this huge wave of black shadows crashes down on everyone, knocking us all down. All I see is darkness and all I feel is panic.

# Chapter 13

I'm able to crawl over to one of the racks to help pull myself up so I can slowly stand. "Is everyone alright?" I hear Jules call out as the darkness is fading away allowing me to see everyone.

I can make out Jupiter crawling on the floor while whispering Willow's name over and over again trying to find her. Mav and Dylan help him to his feet. Looking around the room, I see Jules and Harley standing next to each other, helping each other up. My heart stops as I see Asher is still laying on the ground from the wave of shadows. Feeling stable enough to walk, I make my way over to Asher and let out the breath I didn't know I was holding when I realize he is conscious. I extend my hand out for him to grab and help him to his feet. The movement tweaks my back but all I care about in the moment is making sure Asher's okay. Once he is standing, Asher wraps his arms around me, giving me a bone crushing hug.

"You scared the hell out of me when I saw you fly across the room," He whispers. I hug him tighter while he rests his head on top of mine.

"Oh god, this can't be real. Please no," Mav and Dylan are the only thing holding Jupiter up. If they let go, he will most likely fall back down on his knees. "S-she's gone," he mumbles as tears fall down his cheeks. I have never seen Jupiter like this before and it makes my breath hitch.

Letting go of Asher, I walk up to Jupiter giving him a hug. He holds onto me and I do my best to keep us both standing, taking his weight as I comfort him.

"We'll get her back, it will all be okay," I promise him even though in my heart I know I can't guarantee him this.

"I can't lose her Blue. She means too much to me, I just can't," He rests his head on my shoulder and cries. "I-I think I'm falling in love with her," I was surprised to hear him say this. I knew he may have strong feelings towards her by the way he acts with her, but I didn't know he felt this strongly despite how happy Willow makes him and how comfortable Willow is with him in return. I've noticed that Willow seems to gravitate most toward Jupiter out of the group. I've also caught Jupiter sneaking glances at her in moments when he thinks no one is looking.

"I know we haven't known each other for that long, but from the moment I saw her, I just knew she was different. We talked more when you guys were asleep. I got to know her more and I think that's when I started to fall and I'm falling hard. There's so much more to her than what she lets on. I just can't lose her," Jupiter sobs into my shoulder. I rub my hand up and down his back and say things to calm him down. It worries me to see him like this. No one says anything while I try to help him calm down, giving us space.

Dylan walks away and starts grabbing more weapons from the racks. He walks back over and flips the dagger so the handle is facing out. He holds it towards Jupiter, who just stares at it.

"If we're going to save her, then we can't waste any time," Dylan says. "The more time you spend crying, there's more of a chance of her being gone forever," Dylan's words are harsh but they change something in Jupiter. He stands up, letting go of me, and takes the dagger. Jupiter and Dylan share a knowing look with each other.

After gathering weapons, we head back to my dorm where both Dylan and Jupiter seem to be in their own worlds. Their eyes aren't completely focused on what's going on around them. We finally happen across some guards, and though it's good to know they aren't all dead, we lie to them saying we heard screaming from the training facility.

We don't want them to stop us and ask questions, knowing that would only waste our time, so we don't share that we were the ones who were attacked though if they paid close attention they could probably tell. We make sure to keep our weapons hidden as they run towards the direction of the training facility.

When we get back to my dorm, everyone finds somewhere to sit after we store the extra weapons we brought with us.

"If we are going to get Willow back, then we need to figure out a plan," Dylan announces. It feels odd having one less person here. Emptier.

"We need to find out where the demons would have taken Willow first. Where they have been hiding this whole time," Mav says.

"We know they like dark places, that's a start," says Harley. Harley and I are sitting on my bed, side by side supporting each other in an unspoken way. There is good news that came out of this and it's that no one is hurt too bad, just a couple scratches and bruises. Jupiter seems to be doing better than he was a moment ago, though he could be in shock. My back still feels sore, but I'm guessing it will probably feel like that for a couple of days.

"What if we tried to follow them at night? Maybe one of them can lead us to their hideout? It's a risk putting us in danger if we get caught and, well, killed, but it could also work," I suggest. Everyone seems to be thinking over this plan. Jupiter hasn't said anything this whole time, I can't help but wonder what he's thinking right now. He said he is falling in love with Willow, but now she's in danger and could possibly be dead. I've noticed Dylan has also taken an interest in Willow and has really come out of his shell more since she was taken.

"That's probably the best thing we can do right now. We can try looking later tonight," Mav tells everyone, bringing me back to the conversation. "We can split up into groups so we can cover more ground."

Everyone agrees with the plan and we wait anxiously for it to turn dark. We try to eat when we can, but it is hard to stomach food thanks to recent events and as our anxiety builds as we think about what could be waiting for us tonight. There's a chance some of us may not see the sunrise tomorrow.

The time finally comes when it's dark enough to start the plan. It's only ten o'clock at night, I hope it's late enough to draw out the demons, but in reality, they are always out watching us even if we can't see them.

I partner up with Jupiter while Jules and Mav are together leaving the trio of Dylan, Asher, and Harley.

Before we leave Asher walks up to me and takes my hands in his. "Be careful, okay?" He gives me a soft kiss on my forehead.

"I will," I reply. "The same goes for you," I add as Asher nods his head, letting go of my hands then walks over to his group.

We all say our goodbyes heading out the door. Before we leave, we put on all the black clothes we can find, hoping we won't stand out in the dark like we would with our uniforms on.

"So you and Asher huh? Didn't expect that," Jupiter says as we walk the streets. I'm glad to hear some of his sarcastic self come back.

"I didn't either, it just happened. I know it sounds cheesy but I can't explain it. I didn't realize how I actually felt about him until recently," I confess.

"As long as he makes you feel happy and safe, then I'm happy for you."

I look over at him, he just stares straight ahead in his own world again. "Jupiter," I call. At the sound of his name, he looks over at me. "I'm really sorry about Willow. I didn't realize you felt that way about her, but I'm also happy for you. We'll get her back, no matter what." Jupiter gives me a tiny smile, which I know must take a lot of effort from him right now. I give him a heartwarming smile of my own to hopefully ease his nerves.

When I came up with this plan, I didn't realize how difficult it would be to find the demons. They always seem to be around, but we don't find anything. We search for hours and hours, but by 1:00 am we realize our efforts are futile so we head back to the dorm.

When we get back, we spot Mav and Jules walking inside. They have a disappointed look on their face. Once back in the room, they tell us they didn't find anything either.

"We should go back out and keep looking. We shouldn't have stopped," Jupiter says while getting up from the bed and getting more agitated.

"Sit back down Jupiter," Jules' tone makes him comply immediately. "Everyone here is tired and I bet the others are too. They should be back soon and when they are, we're going to go to bed. Since we'll be in bed, that means you will be by yourself, which is too dangerous. Instead, we'll start looking again tomorrow." Jupiter stays silent, but has a heartbreakingly pained look on his face and he absorbs her words. I know he wants to keep looking for Willow, but Jules is right, he can't go out alone. My eyes are starting to feel heavy. I might be tired now, but I probably won't be able to fall asleep knowing Asher and the others are still out there and if I'm honest, I'm dreading falling asleep. These freaking demons are going to haunt my nightmares forever.

Asher, Harley and Dylan get back around 1:30am and just like Jules predicted, they're all tired. We take our normal sleeping spots, but this time Jules sleeps where Willow normally does.

I lay down next to Asher on the floor where he immediately wraps his arms around my waist and pulls me up against him so my back rests against his chest. I pull the blanket I have over the both of us. We haven't talked about what has been going on between us and I don't know if he thinks of me as his girlfriend or where his head is at. To me, I think of him as my boyfriend now reflecting on the way we've interacted recently makes me feel like we are in a relationship.

"Asher," I whisper.

"Yeah," He mumbles back. I turn around so I am facing him as he opens his eyes to look at me. I move my hand up to his cheek and rest it there. He leans into my touch and rests his hand on top of mine.

"What are we?" I ask as my other hand starts to fidget with the blanket and my eyes end up looking down at his chest. "I mean, do you think of me as your girlfriend? We never really talked about it so I didn't know what your thoughts were," I say.

"Blue, look at me," and I do as he says, locking eyes with his stunning dark hazel ones. "Of course you are. I'm sorry I never communicated that to you. I just thought you knew, but I shouldn't have just assumed that," as he gives me a warm heartening smile. I lean into him and kiss him, showing him that I accept his apology.

His lips are soft against mine and both of my hands move from his face down to his neck of their own volition. Asher's hands tightly grip my waist, pulling me closer to him.

"You're so beautiful," he whispers in-between kisses and I wonder if he can feel the blush spreading across my face at his words. "I'm so lucky to have you as mine," our kiss becomes harder, more intense as Asher's hands start to roam my body.

He kisses his way down my cheek, onto my throat then stopping on my neck. I'm able to catch my breath before he comes back up and starts kissing me on the lips again. Our breathing starts to become heavy and we break the kiss. My cheeks feel flushed and the butterflies are going crazy in my stomach.

"I like you, like, really like you," Asher tells me all breathy. He gives me soft kisses on my forehead, eyelids, nose, cheeks, then on my lips again and I melt into it. "I haven't felt this way about anyone else before," he whispers.

"I really like you too," I give him one more kiss on the lips then snuggle towards him while he tightly wraps me in his arms.

We fell asleep like this, huddled up together. My head on his chest, our legs tangled together. I have no nightmares that night, but instead sleep peacefully dreaming of Asher instead of demons.

WE FOUND NOTHING THE next two days. Every night, Asher and I sleep cuddled together, stealing intimate moments here and there where we can. At one point Harley asks me about how my relationship with Asher came to be and I tell her the same thing I told Jupiter, it just happened. It's true. Times like these can bring anyone together, even people who didn't get along at the beginning.

The third night we head back out again in the same groups as before wandering the university once again looking for any sign of the demons. Jupiter and I stay silent, focusing on our surroundings, searching for anything that might help us find Willow. We're all starting to lose hope, but nobody wants to admit it. Especially to Jupiter. He has gotten more anxious as the days go on. In contrast Dylan has stayed quiet, but he too seems to be losing hope every day that goes by. I don't know what will happen if we don't find Willow or even a freaking demon for that matter. Whenever we hear people getting attacked, we rush towards the commotion, but when we get there, the demons are gone with only the bodies of their victims remaining.

We continue our search walking down an alley, daggers drawn, but find nothing. As we turn around to retrace our steps, I catch sight of a dark figure walking past the alley. Jupiter and I exchange a glance then start to follow it, trying to stay as quiet as we can in hopes that it won't hear us. We are led to a series of campus buildings where our classes are held. I'm curious if there is someone in one of the buildings that the demon is going to find? I can't see any lights from outside where we are walking.

Jupiter and I continue to follow at a distance as the demon wanders through the hallways leading us to one of the bigger classrooms in the building. Jupiter and I take a glance inside the room through the open doorway. All the tables and chairs have been pushed up against the walls, leaving the middle of the room open, but not empty. Instead, the room is filled with demons and at the center is Willow tied to a chair. I can see Jupiter become paralyzed beside me as his eyes find her. I quickly pull him inside while the demon's backs are still to us so we are hiding behind the tables and chairs. We slowly make our way along the wall, away from the door just in case another demon walks in. Eventually making our way to the other side of the room by the windows, we stay hidden the whole time.

We watch as a demon comes out of Willow's body and she takes big gasps of breath. The demon that came out of her body holds his arm up in Willow's direction. She goes completely still in her chair.

"Now that I have a hold on your mind, you're going to answer some questions for me," it says. Willow just sits unnaturally still, staring at the ground. "What is your full name?"

"Willow Teal Jackson,"

"Where are you from?"

"Tanra. I live on a farm with my family."

"I didn't ask if you lived on a farm," the demon says aggressively, causing Willow to flinch. "Do you have any siblings?"

"I have four younger siblings, two brothers, two sisters."

"What would you do if I decided to kill them now? Maybe send some of my demons there to go take a visit to your house?"

Willow's face remains expressionless. "Please, just leave my family alone," she replies monotone. Even while speaking she sounds utterly emotionless.

"You don't get to tell me what to do, I'm Morthil, the demon leader! The most powerful one I must say. And *no one* tells me what to do, especially not a little girl like you!"

Morthil. The flipping demon leader is standing right here in this room, having just been in Willow's body and is now controlling her mind. This is worse than I expected, much worse.

"We know your friends are planning something Willow. What were you all doing in the library together?" Morthil asks.

"We were researching." Willow doesn't seem phased by knowing who is in front of her. I hope she's not aware of what is happening and is trapped in her mind. I can't imagine what horrors she has been through these past few days while we desperately searched for her, especially since she has been in the hands of the one and only demon *leader*. The one thing I don't know is why he wanted Willow specifically or was she chosen at random?

"Researching what?" A smile appears on Morthil's face, a devil's smile, like it knows it's about to get what it wants.

"About-" Willow twitches a little in her seat. Makes me wonder if she's trying to fight for control from within. "About y-you," she goes back to being still. As I look more closely, I can see scratches and bruises on Willow's arms. What have they done to her? Or do we even want to know?

"About me?" Morthil asks sarcastically. "If you wanted to know more about me you could have just asked," as the other demons seemed to laugh at what he said. I didn't realize demons had a sense of humor and it pisses me off.

"Do you know what their plan is?"

"No, we didn't make it that far," Willow seems to twitch again. Is the mind control causing her pain?

"I was hoping you would know their plans so I can distinguish them like the bugs they are, but since you don't, you are no use to us anymore." Morthil faces the other demons as he says, "Kill her, but feel free to have a little fun before you do," and the control Morthil had over Willow's mind seems to vanish. She suddenly looks around with horror written all over her face.

"Please! No, stop!" Willow begs. She fights against the restraints holding her down to the chair.

"It's too bad, only if your friends were here to save you, but obviously they don't care about you anymore," he sneers. He stares at her for a moment then says, "Go on, get it over with," as a demon walks up to her and stops a few feet in front of Willow. The demon raises its arm in what feels like slow motion as Jupiter and I watch as dark magic starts to coil around its hand.

"No!" Willow yells, but before I can think of something to do, Jupiter runs towards Willow and jumps in front of the magic, as it hits him square in the chest.

"Jupiter!" I scream, jumping out of my hiding spot and running in his direction, pulling out the dagger I brought with me as I move, swiftly trying to reach Jupiter and Willow, cutting down demons as I go.

By the door, there is a giant blast of fire that sends a dozen or so demons shrieking and flying backwards as Jules and Mav run into the room. I continue taking down demons that get in my way, Jules and Mav doing the same thing. Jupiter crawls to the chair Willow's in and uses it to help him onto his knees. A sense of deja vu hits me, seeing Jupiter approach Willow. She is saying something to Jupiter but I'm not close enough to hear what that is. He tries his best to untie the ropes that bind her to the chair, but his hands are shaking violently, making it difficult to free her.

Once Willow is finally untied, she helps Jupiter onto his feet but before they can keep moving, Jupiter gives her a passionate kiss on the lips. I'm close enough now to see Willow pull away and say, "I missed you too, but let's get out of here first," as she puts her arm around Jupiter and they help each other to the door.

I watch as a demon comes hurtling towards them and without hesitation Jupiter pushes Willow out of the way moments before he is tackled. Willow screams his name as they go rolling across the floor. I'm about to make my way to him when Dylan comes out of nowhere and kills the demon, Asher and Harley right behind him.

Asher searches the room then stops when his gaze lands on me. His shoulders seem to become less tense and he fights his way over to me. A demon comes tearing after me but I stab it with my dagger before it can attack me leaving only some scratches on my arm before it falls to the ground. Shit, that hurts.

Dylan helps Jupiter to his feet. "Get Willow out of here, don't worry about me. I'll be fine," Jupiter tells him. As Dylan starts to let go, Jupiter begins to slump towards the ground, but Mav is there to catch him before he collapses.

"Honestly dude, you are not fine right now. Dylan, get Willow out of here, I got Jupiter," Mav says. Dylan nods his head then scoops Willow up in his arms bridal style and rushes out the door into the hallway.

Everyone covers Mav as he helps Jupiter out the door, but we won't be able to hold the demons back much longer. I look around the room because I don't know what happened to Morthil, he must have left without us realizing.

Once we are out in the hall, Mav yells, "Blue, come hold onto Jupiter." I hurry and change places with Mav as he and Asher stand behind everyone, facing the demons and send them all up in flames. Jules and Harley lead the group towards the exit. I have no clue how this building is still standing and not on fire.

My arm is throbbing from holding Jupiter by the time we exit the building. Asher and Mav's blast seemed to work because none of the demons are following us out. We find Dylan and Willow anxiously waiting for us outside and the moment Willow sees us, she runs up to Jupiter and flings her arms around him in a desperate hug.

"Not to try and ruin anything, but Jupiter really needs to see a doctor," Mav tells the group. As I look closer at Jupiter, I realize he is very pale and seems to be fighting to stay conscious.

Without hesitation we rush as a group to the healing center, but we don't move as quickly as we feel we need to based on all the injuries everyone has sustained. Asher stays close by my side the whole way there, looking over at me occasionally. It's still dark out so it's not lost on me we could be attacked again at any moment. Feeling on edge, my eyes continue to scanning the area.

Once we reach the healing center and make it inside, a nurse takes one look at Jupiter and ushers him into a room immediately. She tells us to wait here and someone will be out to speak to us about our friend once he's been checked in and a doctor has seen him. All we can do is watch as other nurses and doctors run in and out of the room.

# Chapter 14

They don't allow any of us into the room while they are helping Jupiter. They need to keep the room limited to staff only, but honestly, there are too many of us to be able to fit in there even if we were allowed. Some of the nurses come by and check to see if we need anything, noticing our scratches and bruises and offering to help fix us up. We stay silent as we wait, too deep in our thoughts and worrying about Jupiter to speak. Willow is a mess, but I don't blame her, feeling like one myself. Scooching next to Willow, I wrap my arm around her in comfort. Her head rests on my shoulder as we sit in companionable silence. The same question keeps going through my head. *What if he doesn't make it?* But I try my best to get rid of all negative thoughts.

As the sun starts to rise, they let us into the room where Jupiter's laying unmoving on a hospital bed. He looks sickly pale and has an IV in his arm. The sound of the heart monitor fills the silent room showing the steady beat of his heart. The nurse leaves to give us the privacy we need.

Willow quickly pulls up a chair beside the bed and sits down taking his hand and holds it in hers. She gives him a kiss on the forehead and settles back in her chair. Jupiter tries his best to rest his hand on her face but he can't lift his arm. Dylan looks away, seeming a little heart broken. It almost looks like he's blushing.

"I'm so sorry Jupiter. It should have been me, I'm so sorry," Willow whispers. She gives him another kiss on the cheek. Tears start to run down her face.

"Don't say that," Jupiter does his best to wipe her tears. "I would rather it have been me than you." but that response makes Willow start to cry harder. I can feel my own eyes become teary as I watch the interaction between them, it seems too much like a goodbye.

I've gotten really close to Jupiter these past months, and as I look at him lying in the bed looking so weak and vulnerable, I'm so thankful for him and his friendship. He has become one of my best friends in this short amount of time. I can't lose him now, not after everything we've been through. Asher seems to notice my change in attitude because he walks up beside me and puts his arm around my waist. I rest my head against his shoulder, trying my best not to let the tears fall.

"What even happened?" Harley asks. "How did-why is-what happened?" I can tell her eyes are starting to get teary too. I know what we are all thinking, and I don't like it.

"One of the demons was going to blast Willow and kill her. But Jupiter jumped in front of her, taking the blow," Asher explains.

"I don't want to be a pain in the ass," Jupiter says, "but I don't think I'm going to make-"

"Don't you *dare* finish that sentence. Don't even think about it," Harley interrupts him. Tears are falling down her face. "You can't give up hope that easily."

"Alright, I just wanted you all to be aware," Jupiter replies. He does his best to hide the pain and put a smile on his face. "I can't wait to haunt you guys for the rest of your life," Jupiter tries to laugh but it comes out as a cough.

"You're going to be alright, you hear me? The nurses and doctors here will help you, everything will be fine. I know you're trying to be funny, but you just have to promise me you will fight until the end," I plead as I grab his hand. Jupiter's face becomes serious as he watches my melt down. "Promise me Jupiter," I beg, half sobbing. I probably look like a wild mess right now but I don't care. It feels like my heart is breaking.

"I promise I won't stop fighting," he finally responds. Satisfied, I nod my head letting go of his hand, watching as Willow is quick to pick it up in my absence.

"Why don't some of us go to the library? We can look and see if there is a book that says how to heal him. If we were able to find out they were demons then we should be able to find a way to heal him," Mav suggests.

"There might not be enough time..." Dylan starts to say.

"It's either go to the library or don't do anything at all," Jules interrupts him. "And I for one don't want to sit here and wait for death to happen knowing that there could have been a way to help him. I'm sorry to say this, but you've seen the nurses' faces. They've lost hope." Despite Jules' dropping her voice closer to a whisper as she spoke about the nurses, Jupiter still heard every word she said. I shifted my feet uncomfortably thinking we should have had this conversation outside his room instead of right freaking in front of him.

I look back at Jupiter, to find that he is watching all of us. "I'll hang in there until you all get back. I'll be fine."

"Let's go, but we have to be quick. A couple of us should stay back," I say.

"I am not going anywhere, I'm staying with Jupiter," Willow tells everyone. She is still holding his hands.

"I'll stay with them," Dylan announces, quietly watching them both.

"Alright, let's go," Mav says. We rush out the door and down the hallway. The sun has already risen so we won't have to worry about the darkness and the potential for demons but we have some weapons with us, just in case.

We all run the entire way to the library without stopping. It's an unspoken understanding amongst the group that Jupiter's life depends on if we find an antidote or not. The thought makes me pick up my pace and run even faster. We are all tired, feeling emotionally and physically drained which also makes our magic drained too. We better not run into any demons because I won't hesitate to kill them. I know that's violent and not how I've been managing myself since this whole nightmare started, but I'm not in the mood to deal with them.

We reach the library and run straight to the medicinal section. As we skim book after book, we find nothing that feels applicable to Jupiter and the demon attack on him. I'm scrolling through one of the books about ancient medicine when something catches my eye. The section talks about all these mythical creatures and the antidotes for injuries caused by them. It's just my luck that I come across a page that is labeled demons, the antidote right there. "Got it!" I yell. It is a bunch of herbs that the healing facility should have.

We don't bother checking the book out, but instead take the risk and run straight from the library, back to the healing center. Once we're inside, we get a nurse and show them what we found. We won't know if it will truly work until we give it to Jupiter, but we have nothing to lose knowing the worst thing that can happen is doing nothing as he continues to deteriorate. The nurses get to work creating the antidote right away.

We go back to the hospital room and explain what we found and that the nurses are getting it prepared. I can feel my heart rate and anxiety building because it's clear Jupiter won't last much longer. His movements are lethargic at best and his eyelids appear to be heavy as he tries to slowly open and close them. I take a seat by the bed, across from Willow, as Harley sits next to me. We talk to Jupiter about whatever we can think of, making sure he stays awake.

Jupiter's heart rate is slowing down at a consistent rate and whenever he shuts his eyes, it takes longer for him to open them again.

"You have to stay Jupiter. Stay for us, for Willow, me and Harley. Stay for your sisters, your parents. They still need you, we all do. You need to live for yourself too. There is so much out there that you haven't done or seen yet. I still want to take you to Prusmé to meet my family.

Please don't leave us. Please don't leave me" I am holding his hand, as a plea to him, squeezing his hand tightly. I'm afraid to let go of his hand because it feels like I will lose him forever. Like this connection is the last thing holding him here in the physical world with us. "Someone get a nurse," Asher barks urgently while coming up to me and rubbing my back. Jules responds immediately quickly running out into the hallway, yelling for a nurse.

I try to stay positive but it's getting harder every moment that goes by. Jupiter can't die, he just can't. From the beginning he could always make someone smile even if they were having a bad day. He doesn't deserve this. He can't even see his family because the campus is still on lockdown. I realize no one has even told his family, someone needs to find a nurse to try and contact them.

I can't-" he gasps for breath. I can't help the sob that comes out of my mouth. I'm trying to stay strong for him, even if I don't truly feel that way. "Let's not say goodbye. I hate goodbyes, too depressing. How about, I'll see you on the other side," I clutch his hand tighter. Harley lays her hand on top of ours.

"I'll see you on the other side," Harley whispers. I hate how we can't do anything but sit here and wait for death to claim him.

"Jupiter I-I love you. There is so much I still want to tell you but there is just not enough time," Willow whispers to him.

"I love you too Willow," Jupiter replies while Willow rests her forehead on his before they give each other one gentle kiss. This can't be the final kiss, he is going to make it through this I argue with myself. "I'm so grateful I found you Jupiter," Willow continues, but we can barely hear her as she fights back sobs of her own, tears streaming down her cheeks.

"I don't want to say goodbye or see you later because that means I think you won't make it through this. I believe you're strong enough to live. I don't want to say goodbye," I say.

"Then don't. Just tell me you'll see me later," I look into his beautiful brown eyes that are looking back at me. "That way it's not a goodbye."

"I'll-I'll see you later," I whisper. "Thank you for always putting a smile on my face," Jupiter gives me one of those warm heartening smiles of his, I can't help but give one back.

"You're a pretty good football player even if you don't think so. I wish we would have played together longer but I'm grateful for the time that we did have. Perhaps in another lifetime we'll get to," Asher tells Jupiter. He gives Jupiter a hug and whispers something I can't hear as Jupiter closes his eyes and his body goes still.

Jules comes rushing back in with a few nurses. One of them holding what appears to be the antidote in her hand. I turn quickly to the monitors where I see his heart rate becoming slower as my heart spikes with panic and fear.

"Quickly, he's running out of time," Mav howls. The nurse quickly hurries to Jupiter's side lifting the bottle at his lips so he can drink the antidote. It feels like it takes forever for him to swallow the antidote when he lays his head back down on the pillow and takes a deep breath. Everyone is silent and I realize I'm holding my breath as my heart feels like it's going to beat out of my chest waiting to see what happens. His eyes remain closed while his chest rises and falls slower and slower. This can't be happening, we gave him the antidote! It has to work, I scream in my head.

Jupiter slowly opens his eyes and looks across the room over everyone and our panic-stricken faces. "You men better take good care of these ladies for me," Jupiter starts to choke and he can't seem to get any air in his lungs. And just like that he stops breathing and so does the beeping, replaced by the solid ring of the flatline of his heart. All of us are silent.

Jupiter's dead.

# Chapter 15

It's like everything around me goes into slow motion and turns into a blur. All I can see is Jupiter's lifeless body lying on the bed. His eyes still open. I vaguely recognize the sounds of someone sobbing on the other side of the bed and in my peripheral vision there are nurses holding someone back from Jupiter.

He's gone. Gone and never coming back. The antidote didn't work. It should have worked. We did everything the book told us to do! I don't understand what went wrong.

I don't remember getting up or backing away from the bed. Tears are falling down my face like a waterfall and I can't stop them. There is a hole in my chest where something used to be, that something is Jupiter. I begin to feel numb, it starts in my toes then works its way up throughout my body.

Someone's standing in front of me. They pull me into their chest and tightly wrap their arms around me. "Let it all out. I'm here, just let it all out," they say as I stand there being held, but my arms hanging at my side.

I feel my body collapse into theirs. My legs are unable to hold me up anymore. Asher's face slowly comes into focus as I recognize him as the person holding me. I sob onto his chest, getting his shirt all wet from my tears and snot and who knows what else as I completely lose control of my emotions.

I can hear someone gasping for breath. "Oh my flipping god," Jules says. I look over at her to find that she is staring in shock at the hospital bed where Jupiter lays, seemingly frozen to the spot, her mouth hanging open.

I follow the direction of where she is gaping at the hospital bed and realize the sound I heard of someone gasping for air is Jupiter! He suddenly sits up clutching his heart. "Oh my god!" I scream. Holy shit, he's alive! Alive and choking. I rush towards him but the nurses get to his side first.

One of them positions herself behind Jupiter wrapping her arms around his torso balling her hands into fists placing them towards the top of his stomach and below his sternum as she pulls upwards and backwards at the same time as hard as she can. Jupiter coughs more violently as some of the medicine comes out and he is able to take in big gulps of air. Once he is breathing again the nurse starts asking him questions and starts hurriedly taking his vitals.

He's alive. He's freaking alive.

"We will need to give him some space, everyone. I need you all to back up or leave the room," another nurse says.

Willow blatantly ignores the nurse going straight to Jupiter's side giving him a kiss on the forehead then leaning down to gingerly give him a hug. So much for space, I chuckle to myself as tears of joy and relief stream down my face as I watch her with Jupiter. She whispers something I can't hear and a slow grin spreads across Jupiter's face. After a few minutes I approach him and stand next to the bed.

"You just scared the shit out of me, you know that right?" I say as I give him a big hug but make sure not to squeeze him too hard.

"It appears I did. I'm here now and that's what's important, right?" he replies, seeming to finally take in the scene around his hospital room, noticing everyone's tear-stained faces. I take a step back, letting Harley approach him next.

We all stay in the hospital room and talk to Jupiter for the next few hours while the nurses come in periodically to check his vitals. At one point we go to the cafeteria at the healing center to get some food.

Jupiter dying was one of the worst moments in my life. I felt numb and empty and I never want to feel that way again. Even though Jupiter technically just died, he is somehow still his joking self. I don't know how he does it, how he keeps a smile on his face, especially in a moment like this. I'm just beyond grateful he is still here with us.

That afternoon, they kept Jupiter at the healing center for observation and tests. The nurses asked that only a couple people stay in the room so they have space to help Jupiter. In the end, Willow and Dylan stay with him while the others head back to my dorm building where we all hang out, trying to distract ourselves from what just happened and get some much needed rest. I'm still worried that something is going to happen to Jupiter, but Asher reassures me that everything is fine and if anything were to change, Willow or Dylan would let us know immediately. At one point, the boys go out to get dinner for the group and when they leave, Jules and Harley pounce on me and start asking questions about Asher and I. As they stare at me waiting for details, it feels like everything is normal and we are just a couple of nineteen-year-old girls hanging out, talking about boys...not that one of our friends literally just died in front of us before coming back from the damn dead.

When Asher and Mav get back, we eat our dinner and eventually settle in for the evening passing the time playing cards.

My mind eventually wanders to Luna. I wonder if her family knows what happened? Has her body even been able to be sent home? If it has, have they been able to have her funeral? I occasionally think about Luna and what it would have been like if she was still here. Would we have gotten to know each other better and become best friends? I try not to think about it too much or I start to tear up. I try not to think about any of the events of the last few weeks too much, let alone how many people have died. I wish this was all a bad dream and it was still the night before I left for the university, but it's not a dream, it's real. I just have to think about keeping myself and my friends safe.

After a few rounds of cards, Mav looks back over the books we took from the library. Asher and I sit on my bed, cuddling while I read one of the books Luna gave me. It's crazy how Asher and I went from disliking each other to being in a relationship. I guess enemies to lovers can exist, not that we were necessarily enemies, let alone lovers. If someone told me that Asher and I would be together when we first met, I wouldn't have believed them, but I'm glad I have him throughout this horrible situation.

Harley and Jules are sitting together on the edge of the other bed, talking about how they always like to get their nails done. I've never thought of Jules as someone who gets her nails done, but now I can see it.

Mav continues to flip through a book while lying on the other bed next to Jules and Harley when he suddenly sits up, looking at the book intensely. He's gripping it so tight that his knuckles are turning white and I think he's holding his breath.

"What is it?" Asher asks him with concern in his voice. Everyone is looking at Mav now.

At first, he doesn't answer. His eyes keep moving back and forth across the page clearly reading something with an intensity that is making me on edge. "I think I just found out how to get rid of the demons," everyone starts at his shocking declaration, but he keeps reading the stupid book, not explaining what he found.

"Are you going to tell us or just leave us hanging?" says Jules with a clear edge of frustration to her tone.

"I don't know how I missed it before. You know how Morthil controls all the demons since it's the leader and all that?" he asks, eyes still trained on the book. Everyone nods their heads in unison to his question. "Well, in order to stop all of the demons from attacking us, we have to get rid of Morthil. Its power is what keeps the demons in our world, so if we defeat the demon leader, then the others will return to where they came from," Mav explains with a simplicity that feels too good to be true.

"Which is where?" I ask him.

"Hell," Jules answers for him.

"Yeah," Mav replies. He keeps reading the passages from the book.

If we are going to get rid of these demons, we need to get rid of Morthil. It is the demon leader and its power is stronger than the others. We will need to come up with a good enough plan that will bring Morthil down, because us failing is not an option.

That night I had a hard time falling asleep. My mind is wide awake, running a million miles a minute thinking about how we can defeat Morthil. Jules and Harley are sleeping on the opposite bed as Asher and I. Asher has his arm around my waist, pulling me right up against him, spooning my back against his chest. Mav is sleeping in-between the two beds on the floor. We gave him some pillows and a stack of blankets so he will hopefully be somewhat comfy.

I listen to the sound of Asher's breathing, the feeling of his chest rising and falling and eventually the steady rhythm helps me fall asleep.

THE NEXT MORNING, WE get breakfast then head to the healing center. When we walk into the room Jupiter's staying in, I can tell he's already getting better. He doesn't look as pale as yesterday and he's actually sitting up. The antidote must be helping his healing process. Once we get an update on Jupiter, we explain to the others what we learned from the previous night.

"We were thinking that we could discuss a plan here with you guys," Mav tells them. The nurses let us bring in enough chairs for everyone to sit.

"I want to be involved in this plan too," Jupiter announces. "I feel like I'm capable of participating."

"Please tell me you're joking. You literally just died, then freaking came back to life. No way are you in any shape or form capable of fighting demons right now. You can help with the plan but that's all. End of this conversation," I tell him.

"Listen *mom*," Jupiter says sarcastically. "I'm nineteen, I'm capable of making my own decisions."

"Even if we wanted you to come, no way the nurses are letting you out of here so fast," Dylan says. Jupiter thinks about it for a second then says, "Fine, I'll stay," as he lays back down on the bed and closes his eyes, clearly pissed. I can tell that he is hiding how tired he is and wonder if he got any sleep last night? He should know by now that he doesn't have to pretend to be strong in front of us, especially me.

"If we're going to kill Morthil, we have to draw it out of wherever it's hiding," Asher explains. "Maybe since they were hiding at the school buildings last time, we could base our plan around there."

"That could work. We could maybe stand in the courtyard so they will see us from both buildings," Harley suggests. "Draw them out that way."

"Why don't only a few of you guys stand in the courtyard and just start yelling for them. They may find you as a tasty snack and come out," Jupiter says sarcastically. "Then everyone else could be hiding, waiting for more of the demons to come and ambush them."

"We have to find a way to get Morthil out, he will be our main focus, but we also need to be careful of the other demons," Asher tells everyone.

"We'll use powers and weapons," I say and everyone nods their heads in agreement. I feel bad for leaving Jupiter out, but he almost got killed and I'm not letting him go anywhere when he is this weak, there's no way.

"When are we going to do this?" Willow asks.

"How about tomorrow morning? That way we can prepare and try to get a good night's rest," Jules suggests. Everyone agrees that tomorrow morning is when we make our move.

Looking around at everyone, I try to memorize their faces and how we all look in this moment. I start to remember the times we've worked, laughed and ultimately fought together. We are a team and no matter what happens tomorrow, I'm grateful to know everyone here. Even though I just met most of them, I would call them my family, a family that I can always count on.

# Chapter 16

We spend the rest of the day working through the details of how we want our plan to go. We sort out the weapons we have available to us and distribute them among the group, with Mav and Asher showing us techniques based on the weapons we choose. That night, the nurses release Jupiter from the healing center much to our surprise. It was earlier than we all expected but they said that the antidote helped more than just keeping him alive, it healed him at an accelerated rate, but we still agreed that Jupiter should stay in the dorms tomorrow and away from all the action. We decide to sleep in my dorm again with Asher and I giving up my bed to Jupiter and Willow so he is not on the floor. Even with the events that are going to come, I don't have trouble falling asleep. This could be my last night of sleep and I'm going to savor it.

It's seven in the morning when we get up. We want to get this over with nice and early. The sun has just risen so there shouldn't be many students around since no one has been going to class lately, which we found out at the healing center from the nurses caring for Jupiter. Students have mostly been staying in their dorms except to get food or they are injured and need help.

Once we eat breakfast and arrive at the courtyard, we all take our positions. Asher and Harley are the two who will draw the demons out. It's difficult to see the two people I care deeply about exposing themselves to danger. Once there are too many for them to handle, that's where everyone else comes in. Mav and Asher are going to focus some of their firepower on keeping a protective layer around everyone.

We can only hope that the fire keeps the demons from taking over our bodies, but we haven't had the chance to test this theory. We all feel anxious about the fact that this will all be for nothing if Morthil doesn't show up.

I hide behind one of the bushes with Mav as planned. Harley and Asher wait a few minutes for everyone to be ready. Once they are sure everyone is hidden from view, they walk out into the middle of the courtyard shifting so they are standing back-to-back, weapons ready. We watch from our hiding spots as Asher says something then Harley nods her head.

"Come on out here you bitches!" Harley yells out. I realize I'm holding my breath in anticipation, but there is no response, only silence.

"Are you all afraid to fight us? Or is your leader too afraid to send you out here?" Asher yells. The mention of their leader must have drawn them out because two demons appear from one of the buildings. The demons walk slowly towards them. When the demons get close enough, they easily fight them off with their daggers then Asher burns them. We are going to heavily rely on Asher and Mav because we need them and their fire power in order to kill the demons. As soon as the two demons are dead, more come. My heart is beating faster as more of them come out of hiding. I don't usually see demons in daylight but they are ugly and I reflexively gag.

Harley and Asher don't seem to be struggling much as they fight off the demons, but despite how well they appear to be handling themselves and the five new demons approaching them, I can feel my anxiety growing because Morthil has not come out yet.

"Once a couple more come out, we need to go help them. We are pushing the limits on how many demons they should face alone," Mav whispers to me. A few more demons start to approach from one of the school buildings.

"Are you too afraid to come out here and face us yourself, Morthil? Just sending your minions to do your dirty work for you," Asher yells as he swings his dagger at a demon. It falls to the ground and he moves to his next target. His flame darts towards the injured demons, burning them so they can't come back alive. He stops for a moment, chest heaving and scanning his surroundings before jumping back into action.

"Now." Mav whispers. Without hesitation we run out from the bush towards Asher and Harley. The others that are hiding notice us running to help and join us.

Mav and I fight our way through the demons to get to the others. I do my best when I use the dagger I brought with me. I'm not as experienced in fighting as Mav, Asher or Dylan but I know the basics. I remember the three of them telling me about how they used to have a training yard in Gena.

I don't know how long we try to lure Morthil out but I can tell Asher and Harley are starting to get tired because their movements are slower. I never expected Willow to be the best at using a sword or dagger, but she seems to be holding it together. Jules is like a killing machine, knocking demons down one by one. I don't think I want to know how she learned to fight like that, but what I do know is that I never want to be on the other end of that wrath.

I'm getting sick and tired of waiting for this damn demon leader to come out. "I thought you were the *strongest* demon Morthil!" I yell. "I thought you're supposed to be the great and the powerful one, but all you're showing right now is how much of a chicken you are. You're a big fat *coward*!"

There is a rumble from inside one of the buildings and I desperately hope this means I got Morthil riled up. To my initial relief, but then fear, Morthil walks out with dark shadows circling around it. What the hell?

Morthil yells as it blasts its power right at us, taking out some of its own demons that were in the way. Luckily, we all dive out of the way before its power reaches us. We all scatter to whatever hiding places we can find and Morthil starts to randomly blast its power anywhere it feels we are hiding to try and hit us. I can see the others still fighting other demons that have them cornered a good distance away.

Sweat runs down my neck and back as I try to calm my breathing and focus on what to do next. As I take stock of myself my arms are sore, my legs are starting to ache and I can feel my heart pounding so much, it seems like it will come right out of my chest.

I don't have time to dwell on how I feel as a demon rounds the corner and starts to attack me. As I fight the demon, I hear Dylan yell out in agony and it feels like my heart skips a beat. I kill the demon in front of me and frantically start to look around for him. Once I spot Dylan, I see Asher is already by him as Dylan kneels on the ground clutching his side. Asher protects him by blasting the approaching demons with his fire.

My eyes move away from them and towards a blast of fire in my peripheral vision. Mav is trying to distract Morthil while Jules attempts an attack from behind. As she gets close enough to end it, Morthil spots her and knocks her back with its arm, causing her to go flying through the air and crashing into the ground. Mav tries to blast it again with fire but Morthil is too freaking fast and dodges it. In quick succession Willow approaches from behind while it's still distracted glaring at Mav and throws a huge boulder at it using her earth power. She may seem small and stature but she is fierce. Morthil didn't see this one coming so it doesn't have time to dodge it as we hear the loud crash of the boulder hitting the ground as it crushes Morthil.

Everyone becomes silent, including the demons. We all stare at the boulder that has crushed Morthil. I would have started to celebrate but the only problem is the demons aren't disappearing. Suddenly the boulder explodes so I cover my face to protect myself from the falling debris. When I look up again, standing in the middle of the explosion is the one and only Morthil. Perfect. I should have known that a boulder wouldn't get the job done.

Before it has any time to react, I make another boulder to send its way. It blasts it to pieces with its dark power, the remains falling onto the ground scattering around us in pebbles. It fires its power at me and I barely get out of the way in time. The others start to react and push towards Morthil. Despite their attacks, Morthil evades everyone.

One of the demons comes towards me and I stab it in the chest with ease as Mav burns it before it can get back up. I look back over my shoulder where I last saw Morthil and at that moment Morthil's back is towards me completely unprotected and unguarded. It is too focused on trying to kill the others it doesn't even notice me. In my mind I can imagine Morthil's back is a big flashing target with a sign over it that says "X marks the spot."

It's like everything happens in slow motion. I run towards Morthil as fast as I can, avoiding all the demons that try to block my way. I use my momentum and jump off the ground and come crashing down towards Morthil. It doesn't expect to be attacked from above but damn it. I aim my dagger and stab it straight through the chest. I hit the ground and roll out of the way just as someone hurls fire at it to ensure it doesn't get back up this time. Morthil makes a horrible shrieking sound, so awful that I have to cover my ears. Mav and Asher create a barrier of fire around to keep it trapped where even Morthil's power can't break through.

I watch as Morthil's form starts to fade away into dust. "NOOOOO," it yells as it completely disappears from existence, all the way back to hell. I don't completely register what just happened until I hear the others' cheers. We just killed Morthil, the great and powerful demon leader. And by "we", I mean just a few nineteen-year-olds! I am having a hard time believing it.

The demons around us start to panic as they too start to vanish. Morthil's power isn't strong enough anymore to keep them in this world anymore. All of us stand and watch as each and every demon turns to black dust as they vanish. Without their leader, they are nothing.

Someone places their hand on my shoulder. I turn around to find Jupiter standing next to me loosely holding a sword in one of his hands that is covered in a dark substance. It takes me a minute to fully realize that Jupiter, who is not supposed to be here, is standing next to me with a sword.

"What the hell are you doing here?" I ask, giving him my full attention.

"Well, I couldn't miss all the action," he says as I give him a stern look. "I actually felt the earth start to rumble and I thought something was wrong. So I came here as fast as I could. I couldn't just lay in bed when all my friends could be dying!"

"Well, that was a very stupid and dumb decision!" I jab him in the chest but wince when I remember he almost died and quickly check to make sure I didn't hurt him.

I turn away from Jupiter and listen to the others' cheers with the exception of Dylan who is lying down as Asher appears to be kneeling by him. As I get closer, I can see Asher is actually holding Dylan in his lap. I catch my breath and hesitate as I realize this isn't good. All the others slowly start to notice them as well and it gets eerily quiet.

"No," Mav whispers as he runs over to them while the rest of us approach more cautiously. Mav kneels on the other side of Dylan and grabs his hand.

"There has to be something we can do to help him," Asher says. He removes his hand from Dylan's stomach, his hand covered in blood, to show us the wound. He has tears falling down his eyes as Mav looks over Dylan's injury.

Asher adds pressure to the wound again to slow the bleeding while Mav starts to tear up as he struggles to say, "There is nothing we can do. He's lost too much blood and we won't make it to the healing center in time."

"Don't say that in front of him!" Asher lashes out. "There has to be something we can do. I'm not going to let him die!" I slowly approach Asher so I don't startle him. Once I'm behind him and rest a hand on his shoulder I rub my thumb slowly back and forth trying to comfort him. My eyes are starting to burn as I hold my tears back. Mav is still holding one of Dylan's hands and gives it a squeeze. None of us want to consider the death of a friend again.

"Please don't argue guys," Dylan whispers. He tries his best to take a deep breath. "I don't want to see you both fighting if these are my last moments with you."

"This is not your last moment Dylan. Don't lose hope, please," Asher whispers as he looks up at the others. "Does someone have a jacket or something to wrap around the wound?"

"I do," Harley says as she quickly takes her jacket off and hands it to Mav. Asher removes his hand and Mav does his best to wrap it around Dylan without hurting him. I notice that his hands are shaking while he does this. Once he's done, Harley squats down next to Mav and rests her hand on top of his.

I cautiously sit down next to Asher. I don't want to approach him too fast in case he wants to be left alone, which I would understand if he feels that way.

"I love you guys," Dylan tells Asher and Mav. "I'm so thankful to have been close enough to you both to call you guys my brothers. I'm so grateful for the times we shared and I hope you both feel the same way." I can't help the tears that fall down my cheeks and drop to the ground as I listen to him struggle to get across his feelings towards his best friends.

"Please don't go," Asher begs while holding Dylan's hand tightly, but Dylan doesn't seem to mind. He's probably in more pain from his stomach than for how tight Asher is holding his hand. "Please don't leave us," Asher continues to beg in a whisper.

"I'd stay if I could, but we knew the risks and besides, you won't be alone. You have all of them," Dylan says as tears form in his eyes as he looks around the circle at all our faces.

Dylan takes a moment to pause and look at me. I give him my best smile then he looks back at Asher. "You better take good care of her because I can tell she's a very special one."

I give a laugh that is mixed with a sob while I rest my hand on Dylan's arm. "Thank you, Dylan," I give his arm a gentle squeeze then let go.

"I promise I will. I know you'll be watching over me to make sure I do and I know you'll haunt my ass if I don't." Despite the somber feeling, Asher's comment still makes the group chuckle through their tears and sadness.

Dylan looks at Mav and says, "I'll also be happy and support you too when you choose someone," as he winks at Harley before resting his head back and looking up at the sky then closing his eyes and taking a few slow breaths. With his eyes still closed he says, "I'm going to watch over you two so don't do anything stupid." We can't help ourselves and all laugh a little more. Dylan has never been a very talkative person, but I'm thankful I get to see this side of him as I'm assuming the guys had the opportunity to see.

"And Jupiter, take care of Willow. I trust you to treat her with respect. Ms. Jules, I know you're a strong and independent badass woman, but I hope you allow someone in so you too find love in your life," Jupiter gives Dylan one of his warm-hearted smiles.

"I sure will," Jupiter replies.

"I'll make sure to keep an eye on these goonies for you. Rest easy," Jules replies as she swipes away the tears cascading down her cheeks.

"I love you guys...all of you. I'm forever grateful...I got...to know you all," he barely gets out as we watch the light fade from his eyes and his arms go limp. The moment it happens, Asher lets out all the sobs and tears he was holding in and starts to wail.

I pull him towards me and hold him as he cries, his whole body shaking with the raw sorrow he feels at the loss of his friend. He wraps his arms around my waist while he rests his head on my chest clutching to me as I rub his back and I hope for a miracle to bring Dylan back.

I look around through my teary vision to see Harley and Jules comfort Mav while Jupiter has Willow in a tight embrace as they both cry. I know that Willow and Dylan had gotten very close since the start of school, so I can't imagine how she is feeling right now.

Losing a friend is no joke and I make a silent promise to Dylan in that moment to help these boys and Willow through this. Dylan said it himself, they are like brothers, they were more than friends. I don't know what I would do if I lost Harley, I'd be absolutely devastated. The three boys grew up together having what I imagine as the incredible relationship me and Harley share.

I barely hear it when Mav says, "This wasn't supposed to be how it ends. We were so close to making it, all of us were supposed to get out of this nightmare safely."

We were so close to ending all of this madness when we hit rock bottom once again. Dylan's death is a shock and though we knew there was a risk of getting seriously hurt or even dying, I don't think any of us really thought it would happen. I thought it would be like the novels I read where the characters all get their happy endings.

I have no idea how long we stay here like this. The silence is heavy as we comprehend everything that has happened. At one point Jules says," Someone should probably go look for the principal or some of the guards. I have no doubt they heard the noise. The demons had to have left their bodies so it should be safe now."

"I'll go and Willow, you can come with me if you want," Jupiter volunteers. Willow nods and he takes her hand as they head towards the professors building.

After about ten minutes of sitting and comforting each other waiting for someone to arrive the principal makes an announcement over the loudspeakers. "Attention all students, this is Mrs. Mason. I know that horrific things have been happening for the past couple of months on our campus. Some of you may be confused about the events that have taken place. More information will be shared in detail over the coming days, but I have learned that demons have been haunting Umbra University. Some of you may already know this, but I myself was possessed by one. I ask you to please stay calm and do not panic as these demons have been taken care of so we will be able to take the lockdown order away in the next couple of days. In the meantime, we are going to do a search around campus and we advise all of you to stay in your dorms, only leaving your buildings should you need food. We will be sending medic teams around to help heal the wounded so we need everyone to stay in their dorms until we are able to attend to all students and staff." I don't understand how Mrs. Mason is being so calm, but I guess it's part of her job.

"You are all safe now and we have taken back the University. We will let you all know when you are free to leave. Thank you and if you feel uneasy, unsafe or need support of any kind, please talk to one of the guards or staff members."

I don't understand what she means by *we* but I won't let it bother me. I have more important things to focus on.

LATER THAT DAY, WE get told that the university is sending Dylan's body back to Gena to his family and the place where his funeral will be held. They will have the funeral once Mav and Asher have access to return back home.

Now it's dark out again and we are all back in my dorm room with Asher and I sleeping in my bed. I hold him as he cries and I silently cry with him, occasionally giving him a kiss on his cheek or forehead and murmuring comforting words to him.

"I'm here for you Asher," I whisper in his ear. "I won't let go of you until you are ready, okay?"

Asher pulls me closer to him. "Stay with me," he whispers. "Don't let go."

"I won't," I say as I kiss him on his head. "I promise," I add as Asher lifts his head up and kisses me on the lips, soft and slow. We go back to holding each other and stay like this for the rest of the night.

As we lay in bed holding each other I feel the need to be strong for Asher, despite the heartache I feel at the loss of Dylan and frankly, all the crap that's happened to us over the last few weeks. He's helped me so much throughout all this and I want him to be able to let both let his guard down around me and trust me to be the same support for him that he has consistently been for me. He doesn't need to hold anything back, he can let it all go.

# Epilogue

I stand in the Golden Territory Woods in Gena, many miles away from the University. My family to my right side, Asher and his family to my left. Harley and her family stand with us along with Mav, Jupiter, Willow and Jules.

We stand together, the tall green trees towering over us. The sound of birds chirping in the trees makes its way to us on this beautiful day, the weather is perfect. If only the same could be said for why we're here. Asher and I hold hands, being each other's rock. We're dressed in all black as we face the casket. More specifically Dylan's casket as we say our final goodbyes to him before they lower him into the ground.

Now the speeches are to be made and Dylan's parents approach the burial site to go first. "It is difficult to stand before you here today and try to capture Dylan in these words. Words can't describe my wonderful boy who grew up to become a man," Dylan's parents go on to talk about his childhood and their favorite memories of him. They talk about his dream for the future after University, he wanted to be an architect.

Mav is next to make his speech, then Asher after him. Letting go of my hand he walks up to the little podium that was brought out here. He stands in front of everyone in his black suit and tie. His brown typically tousled hair is all neat and trimmed. He takes out a piece of folded paper from his pocket. After looking over it, he looks back up at everyone.

"There are a lot of things I could say tonight, a lot of things I want to say, but there are not enough words and time to say it all. Instead,

I'll start off with saying that Dylan Pallet is one of the bravest people I know. He never expressed his fear as we fought the demons or as he ran towards danger. Most men I know would have run away. He put his life in danger so we could all be here today. Dylan knew there was a chance he might not come out of the fight alive, but that didn't stop him.

"Just like he was never afraid when we would go searching the woods when we were younger. He was always the clever one out of him, Mav and I, but he would never make fun of us for being ourselves and that's one of the things I love about him. He had courage and a kind heart. He's the type of person I want to make proud and inspire to be like. He is my friend, my brother, and my family. I will never forget him, he will always have a place in my heart. So Dylan, if you are listening, know that I miss you and I will forever cherish our memories. And I'll keep to my promise."

Asher folds the paper and puts it back in his pocket. The crowd applauds him as he walks back to me. He wraps his arm around my waist and plants a kiss on my temple. My eyes are puffy and red from all the crying I've done, yet somehow there are still tears falling down my face.

Dylan was brave for fighting that day, we all were, but he was the true hero. He gave up his life and fought to protect others.

I'm so grateful I got to meet him along with all the others. I don't know who or where I would be without them. One thing I know for sure is that I wouldn't be the person I am today. Every student at the university has been through so much and it will take some time for us to heal, but all this has made us stronger.

The demons may come back one day, but this time we will be prepared. We know our enemy and we know their weaknesses. The Andagar Realms are not afraid.

## Acknowledgements

TO MY MOM, THANK YOU for taking the time to sit down with me to help edit my book and provide feedback, even when you had a lot going on. My book wouldn't be where it is today without your guidance.

To my dad, who read my book, even though he's not a huge reader, and provided feedback from an outsider's perspective. Thank you for all of your love and support.

To my brother, Logan, who's excitement and encouragement has made me even more excited to share my story with the world.

To Jenny Leitsch, you helped me believe in myself as a writer and your encouragement has motivated me to not be afraid to share my story. Thank you for helping edit my book and for believing in me.

To my friends and family, thank you for all of your wonderful support. I'm so grateful to have you all in my life and I'm so excited to share my story with you.

To Becky Smetak, thank you for bringing my book to life by making the cover I dreamed of...and your patience for all the various versions I asked for.

To Ayla Myers, thank you for the beautiful author photo. I enjoyed our photo session together.

And finally, to the reader, thank you for giving my book a chance and sticking with it until the end. You are what motivates me to continue to write stories, so I can share the worlds and characters with you. I hope you enjoyed Blue's story as much as I enjoyed writing it.

# About the Author

Ella Kyle is an eighteen year old senior in high school. Since the age of six, Ella has loved creating stories, whether that be cardboard covered books or plays for her and her friends to perform. Her favorite genre to write is fantasy but dystopian comes in a close second. She's actively involved in school life including track & field, National Honors Society and orchestra. She also loves to help out and volunteer for her community. Ella is an avid reader and loves to spend her time outdoors and being active. She loves a good creamy mac and cheese, but also can't resist a delicious cookie cake. She plans to start working towards a degree in Creative Writing to continue her dream of being an author.

9 7 9 8 2 2 4 8 7 6 8 2 2